I0764338

The FOUR APOSTLES

Book II

A Breath Away

J. Judson Lacko

THE FOUR APOSTLES: A BREATH AWAY

This book is written to provide information and motivation to readers. Its purpose is not to render any type of psychological, legal, or professional advice of any kind. The content is the sole opinion and expression of the author, and not necessarily that of the publisher.

Printed in the United States of America.

ISBN 978-1-949746-91-4 (Paperback)
ISBN 978-1-949746-92-1 (Digital)

Lettra Press books may be ordered through booksellers or by contacting:

Lettra Press LLC
18229 E 52nd Ave.
Denver City, CO 80249
1 303 586 1431 | info@lettrapress.com
www.lettrapress.com

Contents

Chapter 1

Crisis

The secure phone line had a red button set into the base of the phone, which would flash in times of crisis. If depressed, that button would automatically connect the phone to the White House Rapid Response Center. At exactly 0200 hours on (Sunday, October 12th 2008) the line went hot. Jack Logan was still half asleep when he reached over and picked up the phone, pushed a similar red button on his phone.

"Jack Logan, ID 374," he said.

"Jerry Whitfield, ID 177," a man replied. "...Eagle (the President) wants everyone associated with this briefing, code name 'Operation Blue Light' to assemble in the Rapid Response Center ASAP. The Four Apostles Project has been compromised. A coded message sent to a terrorist group headquarters in Lebanon by one of their operatives here and was intercepted by the CIA. The message speaks of appending military action that could end up destabilizing the entire Middle East, resulting in big problems with our allies there. The briefing begins at 0300 hours. Better bring some coffee, Jack. It's going to be a long night."

With that, the phone went dead. Jack looked at the receiver, and replaced it in its cradle, wiped the sleep out of his eyes and got out of bed.

Jerry Whitfield, the White House Chief of Staff, had sounded forboding, to say the least. Jack, as the new Director of Middle East Strategic Operations Services Group, had only been briefed on his duties the day before. The preparation for The Four Apostles Project spanned almost two decades, and held the highest level of federal secrecy and Jack knew that that briefing was just the tip of the iceberg. He still didn't know what he didn't know but the level of pending information he would soon learn would be far and beyond what Jack could have imagined.

Jack hurriedly dressed, kissed his sleeping wife on the forehead, and rushed down the stairs and out to his car where the cool autumn air further woke him up.

As he turned from his driveway onto the cul-de-sac, the headed toward the Beltway driveway on to the cul-de-sac, then towards the Beltway, Jack was aware that more secured lines were going hot, as they always did for the personnel associated with a crisis and Jerry Whitfield was activating more red button phones as Jack headed for the White House. Operation Blue Light, as it would be named by the Joint Chiefs of the Military Staff, was coming alive.

Jack reached the White House forty minutes later, flashed his security pass at the security guard who knew him well, and was directed to a secured parking area. He entered the White House by the side entrance, and two Marines escorted him to the Rapid Response Center. Jack surveyed the room as he entered, before taking his assigned seat at the long oak wood table.

Two men were talking in low tones at the far end. They glanced up at Jack as he seated himself, and then resumed their quiet conversation.

Classified documents rested on the table in front of each chair bearing the usual security seal, 'For Authorized Personnel only Top Secret'. They would remain sealed until the Chairman of National Security instructed everyone in the room to open them.

By 0300 hours, after all thirteen participants, including the President, had entered the Rapid Response Room, and the doors had been closed and locked. The Chairman. Jim Wells, National Security Chief, opened the session.

"Gentlemen, I thank you all for responding so quickly at such an early hour, Jim said. "However, I'm sure you will soon appreciate the sense of urgency. This briefing has been called because of the files in front of you. Please open them"

A rustling of papers was heard as the files were removed for examination.

Wasting no time, Jim continued. "About four hours ago, United States operatives in Lebanon intercepted a coded message to a terrorist group headquarters operating from within Lebanon. The message directed the group to prepare for an unparalleled military attack against Israel, if Israel does not immediately halt building Israeli housing on the West Bank, and if the United States does not withdraw its Navy and ground forces from the Middle East.

Jim paused, for a moment giving everyone in the room a chance to catch up.

"When the United States and Israel receive this proposal, their two governments will have two weeks to comply and issue a favorable response. We estimate it will take five to seven days for them to set this up.

"This terrorist group, known as the Scorpion Brigade, intends to start World War Three."

Bob Howell, the Director of the Central Intelligence Agency spoke up.

"Are we absolutely sure these terrorists have the new sequencer initializer and can use it as a pre-emptive strike device? My people have no proof this threat exists."

"Oh, it exists," came a voice from the other end of the table.

"May I say something, Mr. Chairman?"

Jack realized the voice belonged to one of the two men he had noticed having a low toned conversation when he first entered the room.

"By all means, Professor Ramsey." the chairman replied.

"Gentleman, this is Professor Peter Ramsey, Director of the Four Apostles Project. He-s the most qualified to speak on the current situation."

Professor Ramsey pushed his chair back taking his place at the head of the table. He adjusted his glasses, and gently pushed back his greying hair on the right side of his forehead.

"To understand the current crisis, we go back to the initiation of the project," Ramsey said. "This began during the during the past White House Administration. By Executive authority, two plans were authorized: The first one would insure national protective action against foreign attack: the second plan was to protect our energy interests in the Middle East by providing a contingency plan to occupy certain parts of the Middle East, should the need arise. Both plans were initiated. Both plans were leaked to the public and opened to public scrutiny."

Ramsey pulled the Strategic Defense Initiative map photographs for each plan from his folder and placed them on the table in front of him.

"By the time the SDI plan was discovered and exposed," Ramsey said, four operational laser platforms had been built and tested and were ready to be launched into space. Congress had not been entirely briefed on the readiness of the system nor its pending launch into space and the programmed orbit. Cost for the project seemed prohibitive, and the general public was hesitant to fund another military project without further scrutiny. For all intent and purposes the project was scrapped- or so Congress and the public were lead to believe."

"The second plan involving the occupation of certain areas of the Middle East. should our energy interests in that region be threatened, was devised to prevent economic chaos and collapse of the American economy. Once this strategy was leaked. our Israeli and Arab allies in the Middle East refused to agree to the idea of foreign armed forces occupying their sovereign territory. This strategy plan was put on hold, and our allies tended to relax. This, unfortunately, was not the end of the plan."

Admiral Tyson McNay, Naval Chief of Operations had questions about the plans.

"Mr. Chairman, who would have the responsibility of activating these satellites? And which branch of service would be controlling and maintaining the hardware involved? And what about the costs? A new training center and test site would have to be built. This could cause further escalation of an arms race, since we would have our satellites already in operation. We must consider the consequences of these actions. And then there's' ,,,,

General Carl Mason, Air Force Chief of operations cut McNay off.

"The Air Force would be responsible in a joint partnership with NASA." replied Mason.

"A training center is already being built, and the testing sites are several small islands we've secured."

Innuendos were being uttered under the breaths of the Chiefs of Operations of all the services, but all seemed to agree that the laser platforms were going to be needed to control the Middle East unrest at some point.

Army General Mark Rhodes, Chairman of the Joint Chiefs of Staff, spoke up.

"Gentlemen, each of the armed services will have a part to play in this. The Air Force will take the lead with NASA in coordinating the roles each service. Intel is vital to this project. We must be ready to react to a crisis situation. At this moment, our Intel shows that the factions involved aren't working together to produce a united front against our forces. Since we intercepted the threat, things seem to be changing. If Israel is attacked, we have to respond."

Professor Ramsey withdrew additional data sheets from his folder with satellite data attachments.

Professor Ramsey continued.

"The President didn't want to relax his views on these plans, and arranged top secret meetings with the Israeli government to put a compromise plan in place. The plan called for no actual occupation of the territory of the Middle East countries, but a series of satellites armed with Cobalt lasers would keep a constant surveillance on the Middle East, and would be activated in the event of an attempt to seize territory by a hostile state. Israel agreed to this as long as they worked jointly with American scientists to perfect the laser platforms, and have joint access to the satellites' operational system. The President baulked at the idea of having Israel in the loop' so to speak, in the activation of the lasers, but he finally agreed"

"Professor Ramsey, are you saying that this plan with the Israeli government was implemented without Congress or anyone else in our government knowing about it?" Jerry asked.

Professor Ramsey nodded slowly.

"There is a lot more to this situation, however."

"Israel sent its top physicist, Professor David Goldschmidt, to the United States to work with our own top physicist, Professor Harry Goring. Together they worked out a formula to regulate the intensity of the laser we propose using in this project on a target called the Cobalt Blue process."

"This cobalt Blue process", Jack interjected, "What are the hazards on the ground, once the laser has hit the targeted area? Is there a radiation concern? Would our allies or United States troops be able to function in the battlefield once the laser blast hits?"

"Allow me to explain the process," Ramsey began.

"In that process, Argon gas acts as a catalyst or facilitator for the cobalt beam being passed through the proton accelerator. By controlling the amount of Argon gas that the beam is exposed too, the strength and width of the beam is determined. Ground monitors will then activate the beam to neutralize the target. Troops on the ground will be able to engage the enemy with only a small amount of radiation. As you can see, this will allow for a controlled blast from the laser, limiting or expanding the strike area.

Ramsey paused, slightly stroking his beard, before his cool green eyes met with at least six other pairs of eyes in the room, on at a time.

"Gentlemen, this is now the ultimate weapon"

A full five seconds of silence filled the room before all hell broke loose. Questions were coming from each of the armed services representatives sitting around the table. The Navy Chief of Operations asked about fleet deployment. Was there an additional fleet needed for this project? Did the United States have the allied enough to depend on support logistically and politically should a confrontation occur.

The Army Chief of Operations was concerned about armored transport to the target area tactical support from the Air Force.

The Marine Chief of Operations, General Jason Barkley, voiced concern about recon unit priorities. This would be a new form of combat for them and need assessment.

After a few minutes, General Rhodes called for order, and the questions and discussions came to a halt.

Rhodes turned slowly in his chair and faced Ramsey.

"Are you telling us that Hamas and the PLO have control of the satellites?"

Ramsey hesitated, then responded.

"Not exactly. A break-off faction, known as the Red Scorpion Brigade, possesses the capability to use the satellites but only if they can activate the new algorithm in the Ultimate Sequencing Unit. This is the key component for operating the lasers on the satellites."

Ramsey further elaborated.

"When the system was designed, there were two encoding devices which were set to task the satellites and activate the lasers. Both units have to be brought on line simultaneously in order for the system to operate. If the sequencer is duplicated without the new algorithm, the laser is deactivated, and useless."

"We feel that the people who stole the sequencer and kidnapped Professor Goldschmidt have become aware that the new algorithm will be able to produce a compliment system enabling the satellite lasers."

"What would occur if the terrorists duplicate the system rather than compliment it?" asked General Rhodes.

"The system would require resetting the base in the United States before it could be fired." Ramsey responded.

President Steele entered into the discussion.

"Do any of our intelligence agencies know where Professor Goldschmidt is being held?"

Jerry Wells, National Security Chief, answered the President.

"Intel indicates he is being held in the Libyan Desert, in an old bunker with the security of a small fort. We can easily neutralize it with a bunker bomb."

"Didn't Omar Kaddafi use that once?" asked Logan.

"He did," responded Wells, "When the United States Air Force was sent on a secret mission to neutralize Kaddafi after he had several of our troops, tortured, beheaded and strung up in a market place. Unfortunately, they were unable to locate the bunker at the time. Our on-site intel lacked reliability, and gave us false information."

The President looked at the electronic maps of the desert on the table display panels.

"That's pretty far into the country. Are you sure our special operations team can handle that distance for an extraction?" he asked.

Jack looked down at the maps, and traced with his finger, the route the extraction team would have to take.

The bunker is about three hundred miles south of Tobruk. The extraction team will be dropped just east of there, and work down along the Egyptian border. The transports will be four of the Ghost Shadow Squadron. We now use these stealth helicopters for night excursions into hostile territory. An AWACS aircraft will be above them scanning for hostile response. The helos can come in between fifty and one hundred feet flying with terrain radar for about three hundred miles, while using jammers to thwart the local ground radars. They are capable of carrying a full load of armament and six men per aircraft. Since only three Spec-Ops will be on each of the helos, the travel distance is almost twice as great. Once they arrive at the designated target area, they will land one half mile from the bunker and the Spec-Ops team will move into position. According to our info, the west wall of the bunker be the easiest to breach. When that happens, this team will neutralize any hostiles and move into the bunker. Then, gaining entry, finding where Professor Goldschmidt is located will be their sole responsibility."

"Once Goldschmidt has been located, The Team Leader will signal the Ghost Shadow Squadron to move within seventy-five feet of the bunker. Any additional hostiles will be neutralized, and Goldschmidt will be extracted to one of the helos. Touchdown to dust-off should be within eight to ten minutes of the breach. The helos will then exit northwest of the bunker through a valley that extends to the coast, then fly out to the carrier."

Jack interjected instructions from his end.

"Any part of the coder assembly is top secret. There are ways that the coder can be re-assembled and activated by studying the components. That's why we must make sure that any parts are not left behind. If firefight with additional hostile forces- the coder or its parts are to be destroyed with C-4 high explosives.' The room went silent until Jim Wells continued the briefing.

"There's one difference with this operation, gentlemen, from our usual protocol. We have a special back-up plan in place should we fail in extraction efforts. If the team cannot secure the target, a high altitude bomber that will be circling the site, will release a bunker buster. The target, and everything within one hundred foot area will be destroyed.

General Rhodes turned to the President.

"Excuse me, Mr. President, but don't you think the Israeli government will take a dim view of killing one of their scientist? Especially this particular scientist?" President Steele responded.

"The Israelis have no knowledge of this back-up plan," President Steele stated. "However, just as we do, they recognize that this weapon could bring on a full scale nuclear conflict. Plan B will only be used if all else fails."

The members of the Rapid Response Team discussed the mission among themselves for the next ten minutes.

Finally, Whitfield brought the discussions to a close.

"I don't need to remind anyone here that this is of the highest priority and as such. is not to be discussed outside this room," he said. "Operation Blue Light is now in play effectively starting the clock on our plan."

Chapter 2

Extraction Team

National Security Chief Jim Wells held back watching the rest of the team e the briefing. He walked over to Jack who was reviewing the mission's maps on the electronic board.

"You know who will lead this mission, don't you?" Wells asked.

"Yeah," Jack answered, looking up from mission board. "Why? Is there a problem 'with him taking Lead?"

Wells knew that Jack and his older brother, J.D. always went into a mission as a team. They shared a special bond, not only as brothers, but as brothers in arms. All the cards had to be on the table. No surprises.

Wells looked down at the table, seemingly hesitant about speaking. Then he looked Jack directly in the eye.

"J.D. won't like the idea of a bunker bomb backing him up," Wells said with a slight sigh, "He prefers all his missions with a minimal loss of life, and one thing I intentionally omitted from the briefing was that Israeli commandos will more than likelv trv to do what we are. We could have a collision between the two groups. The U.S. forces have to keep their focus on our mission. If the Israelis interfere..." Wells voice trailed off. "Need I say more?"

Jack slowly stood up and withdrew from the table. He didn't expect this.

"I realize what you're saying, Jim," Jack said, "But J.D. has been backed up by the Israelis on a number of occasions, and what you are inferring will go against the grain with him. He won't take it well."

Wells gather up his briefing notes and returned them to his file folder, placed them in his briefcase, and headed for the door. He stopped just before exiting the room for a last comment to Jack.

"He may have no choice if things 'go south. Perhaps you can talk with him before he joins his unit." Then Wells was gone and heading back to the White House while Jack wrestled with his last words.

Jack would have to talk with his brother, but he didn't have to like it. Not one bit.

Chapter 3

Conflict Within

Jack left the briefing Room trying to figure out how to convey the message he was assigned to give to his brother. After driving through the White House gates- Jack headed towards J.D.'s condo, just a few minutes away.

Halfway there, Jack called J.D. on his cell. The phone rang four times before his brother answered.

"Hey Jack, what's up? You know that this time of the morning I'm either just getting up or turning in.

"What is it this time, J.D. who's giving you breakfast?" Jack asked, laughing. What's her name?'

There were some muffled sounds in the background, some laughing before J.D. responded.

"Give me a break, man. It's just a good friend. I met her last night."

Jack hated to break up his brother's romantic interlude, but, as always, it was the mission first.

Meet me at "Chuckburgers" and we'll have breakfast. See you in ten minutes." Jack hung up before J.D. could protest.

'Chuckburgers' was code used when the two brothers wanted to arrange a meeting to discuss things they didn't want prying ears or electronic devices to hear. There were a series of parks around Washington, D.C. and the day of the week corresponded to the location where they would meet. That would be the meeting point for that day. Both brothers' cars were outfitted with an electronic deflected coated mesh covering the body and a clear mesh on the windows. Radio waves, UHF, UV, or IR waves left the inner passenger compartments impenetrable to listening devices.

Jack arrived first. J.D. arrived a few minutes later, got out of his car and slipped into the front passenger's seat of Jack's car.

"Okay. Jack. What's so important I'm missing breakfast. Not to mention dessert." J.D. said with a chuckle.

"Sorry about that, bro, but your tasty little dish will have to wait." Jack gave J.D. an indulgent smile. "The national security guys have another mission for your team. but it is a slightly different from what you are use to."

J.D. looked intrigued. "Different how?"

"Well, to start with, in addition to you, eleven Spec-Ops guys for the extraction team. But your back-up will be a high altitude fighter-bomber carrying a bunker buster" Jack watched his brother's face carefully.

J.D. starred out the front window.

"How come the extra hardware? Don't they think we can pull off the extraction?"

"You may end up in the middle of 'friendly fire' Jack replied.

"We're not sure what to expect in this case. We do know the target must be removed or neutralized. And we think the Israelis will be in the area to perform their own extraction. The White House doesn't want any interference with this mission." Jack swallowed hard. When he spoke again, his voice was steady and showed no sign of emotion. "If we have to, well, you know the implication."

J.D. gave Jack a sideways glance.

"They never say it, do they? They're in D.C. making all these decisions about how we're to carry out their operations. But I don't think they have any concept of what goes on. It's just a place on a map with a bunch of data on a target. The powers that be have no idea of the impact these missions have on the people who carry out the orders."

Jack turned slightly and looked towards the sun slowly rising. His thoughts drifted back to other missions he and J.D. had been involved in. One in particular was when Jack was sent to Libya to obtain intel on a new type of ground-to-air missile and fire-control system the Libyans were installing in their Mirage fighters. Jack had obtained what he needed and was attempting to leave the country by way of the desert, when he came under attack by two half-tracks. Jack's truck was taking fire from the rear on both sides. Suddenly, three helicopters skirted the sand dunes and appeared in front of Jack's truck, and headed for the hostile half-tracks.

The helicopters open fired on the half-tracks with fifty caliber machine guns and neutralized the threat. Jack stopped his truck and waited for the first helicopter to land.

"Get what you needed?" a Spec-Ops trooper yelled to Jack as he exited the helicopter. It was Jack's brother, J.D.

"How the hell did you know where to find me?" Jack yelled back as he approached the helicopter.

"There was a security leak from one of the locals on our payroll. He saw you coming out of the Libyan Combat Control Center, and radioed the perimeter guard. We, fortunately, were monitoring the radio frequency and took off as soon as the alert came through. After that, it was a piece of cake. You know this is the second time I've saved your bacon!"

The two men boarded the helicopter, and took off toward the carrier waiting for them in the Mediterranean Sea.

Jack's thoughts faded as J.D. continued talking.

"I've been on at least three missions where the Israelis have been a major factor in the successful completion of the assigned op at the time," J.D. said. But 'they were never there', like us. How can they ask us to do something that makes a mockery of what has to be done?"

Jack looked back at his brother.

"Then you'll have to make sure it doesn't come down to that, J.D. Assemble your team at the mission launch point by 0900 hours where they're to be transported to the U.S.S. Enterprise. It's heading for the Mediterranean Sea. I'll see you when you get back."

Jack and J.D. gave each other a 'football hug'

"Stay safe, J.D.," Jack whispered to his brother and J.D. got out and returned to his car and headed for the mission launch point.

"J.D., if you want me to, I'll be glad to go back to your place and make sure your 'friend gets breakfast."

J.D. just shook his head.

"That'll be the day when I send a 'suit' to do what only a Spec-Op Specialist can do."

Jack saw the grin on his brother's face as he got into his car and headed back to his billet to complete his 'assignment' Jack had interrupted.

Jack drove on to the Pentagon, where he was to report for a briefing that would outline the covert operation.

Chapter 4

Operations Underway

President Steele was having his morning Cabinet meeting at 1000 hours, same day, when one of his National Security agents leaned over and whispered into his ear.

The President immediately dismissed the Cabinet, picked up the receiver on his desk phone button and pressed the flashing button. Israeli Prime Minister Benjamin Cohen was on the other end of the line.

"Good morning, Prime Minister. I was told it was urgent," the President said.

"It is, Mr. President. I understand you're planning a visit to our side of the world. Why weren't we informed you were coming?"

The President, who had taken a seat, began to explain.

"We aren't planning on visiting your country, Prime Minister…

"We are well aware of that, Mr. President," the Prime Minister said, cutting him off, "but you will be visiting a close neighbor, and we wouldn't want your presence to cause strained relations with them"

"I don't think that will be a problem, Sir. The visit will be very brief."

The tension on the line was palpable.

"We plan to visit the same place, just so you know. Are we clear on that, Mr. President?" the Prime Minister said. "We want to avoid any problems with our two groups."

The President was annoyed with Prime Minister Cohen.

"We'll have to make sure that doesn't happen, won't we?" he said

"Yes, Mr. President," the Prime Minister replied. "We will both see to it. Good-by, Mr. President."

"Good-bv Mr. Prime Minister," President Steele said, placing the receiver back in its cradle. He immediately told his secretary to page Jack Logan.

"Right away, Mr. President. Shall I direct his call back to your office?" the secretary asked.

"Yes, As soon as he calls back," he said.

Chapter 5

Operation Blue Light Begins

Jack's pager went off just as the Operation Blue Light meeting finished up.

Jack hurried to the back of the room to one of the secured lines and called the White House. President Steele picked up immediately.

"Jack Logan, Mr. President," Jack said.

President Steele's next words show that, so this GWS (goes without saying) "Jack. our team needs to be on high alert for this mission. Our Israeli friends are also going to attempt a rescue. Prime Minister Cohen made it clear they are going to handle this since Professor Goldschmidt is an Israeli citizen, and because of his top status."

"Doesn't the Prime Minister realize that 'friendly fire' could result if the two groups try to outguess each other during this extraction operation?" Jack asked.

"He knows, but his issue is more territorial than operational." President Steele said. "Contact the Joint Chief of Staff and have him send an encrypted message. flash traffic, to the Enterprise alerting them to the situation.

Jack shook his head in frustration. He knew this was going to be a major problem. with two elite teams headed into harm's way, both hoping to resolve the situation.

"Yes. Mr. President. I'll see to it right away.", as Jack headed for the Joint Chief of Staff office. It didn't take long for the Chairman of the Joint Chiefs of Staff to get the message to the Enterprise.

Chapter 6

Helo Prep and Mission

When Senior Petty Officer J.D. Logan's team landed on the flight deck of the Enterprise, it was zero dark thirty, and pitch black outside. Only the sound of waves crashing told J.D. he was on board the aircraft carrier. The twelve-man team was lead below deck to the Ghost Shadow Squadron Ready Room. Their gear was stored in a locked room in the back.

J.D. was reviewing the maps of the extraction area, making mental notes of the positions of the structures on site, points of entry into the structures, and breaking down assignments for the men. The eleven men and himself, would be divided into four squads. He would lead squad one, with Lance Corporal Bill 'Swamp Rat' Douglas serving as his second in command. J.D. knew that bogs and swamps would pose no problem for 'Swamp Rat' , having been raised in the backwoods of Mississippi. He also knew the 5' 9" hard charger with rock hard muscles could quickly infiltrate enemy compounds and subdue the enemy.

Pettv Officer I st Class Jim 'Bagger' Scopes would make up the third member of their squad. A self-proclaimed survivalist, the 5' 10" country boy camping in the hills of Kentucky and learning survival techniques from the age of eight. J.D. knew he could set the best bobby traps around, creating an ambush that would brook no escape.

Squad two would be lead by a 6'3" USA Specialist Five Bret 'Hoops' Conrad, a former New York City basketball star. His agility and fast moves on a basketball court, coupled with his ability to leap further into the air than the best players proved invaluable to his team when he was leading assaults uphill on rising terrain against an enemy position. J.D. knew he could handle dessert terrain of shifting dunes of varying heights to achieve an objective.

Second in command was Petty Officer 2nd Class Joe 'Doc' Morrison. He was the corpsman for the team. He had trained in the paramedics in civilian life, and worked with a hospital that was on the cutting edge of trauma cases and trained their paramedics in triage, suturing, administration of drugs, advanced life support, tracheostomies, and methods of preservation of severed limbs. If there was any way to cheat death in the field, Joe Morrison knew about it.

Pettv Officer 2nd Class Pauley 'Preacher' Vance was third man on squad two. Vance was the conscious for the group. His job was to keep focus not only between the men, but on the missions assigned. "Leave no man behind" was his motto. both on a battlefield or in the minds of the men.

Pettv Officer I st Class Tony 'Badger' Carducci lead squad three. Carducci could bury himself and his squad in any terrain imaginable. Enemy soldiers could walk beside or on top of one of his men, and never know it. His skill at eluding the enemy and sniper assignments were a major asset on any mission.

Petty Officer 3rd class Rich 'Box Cars" Owens was the chance taker in the group. This made him perfect for certain missions. He felt if the odds of an outcome were Fifty-fifty in any situation, not doing the job gave the situation a zero chance of success. With this mind set, his actions in combat somehow seemed to always to produce results favorable to the mission Owens wore a set of dice around his neck on a mission "Snake eyes' were never an option for his group.

Lance Corporal Jose 'Fixer' Gonzales was the third member of squad three and responsible for maintenance on ordinance for the mission at hand. He saw that every man on the team was fully outfitted with equipment relative to the combat situation they were assigned.

Petty Officer 3rdClass Owen 'Nitro' Hicks was lead for squad four. Hicks was a mid-Pennsylvanian farm boy, who loved clearing land with explosives. His father had him setting dynamite charges when he was eight years old. Hicks liked electronics, so he trained in the military how to couple electronic detonators to high explosives using what ever he could scrounge for a detonator. He was the McGyver of the team.

Petty Officer 3rd Class Carey 'Chess King' Parsons worked with J.D. prior to the missions to strategies and establish the equipment list needed for the mission. Parsons was a national chess champion, and studied war tactics from writings by General George S. Patton and General Erwin Rommel. Parsons believed that the success of the battle came from both sides of the combatants.

Pettv Officer 3rd Class Jake 'Whopper' Jordan was the third man on squad four. Jordan had the ability to locate or procure food, no matter what the circumstances were. Jordan got his nickname by obtaining forty hamburgers from an enemy kitchen supply refrigerator during a firefight. This had nothing to do with the assigned mission.

After J.D. set up the assignments, he gathered his men together in the briefing room and stepped to the podium-

"Each squad will contain three men, all of whom will board one of the helos. Make sure all equipment is ready and operational by the time we touch down at the extraction point. Flight time will be approximately one hour. Your maps and compasses should be readily available."

J.D. paused, debating how he was going to explain to his men how this mission was going to be different than other missions. He looked up from the podium and scanned the faces of those who would have to accept this mission.

"This mission is a little bit different than that we normally do," J.D. said. "For example, we might come into contact with the Israelis. Should that happen, remember they are our allies, and not the enemy. We may have to work with their team to complete the extraction. Now, they don't know we're coming, so make sure of your target. The last thing we want is a 'friendly fire' incident.

Owens spoke up.

"How are we suppose to know the difference between the hostiles and the Israelis, Chief? Even with night goggles on, we may not be able to tell. Both sides will be wearing camouflage uniforms."

J.D. responded.

"The Israeli commandos have no special uniform markings, so we're going to have to try using the coded sequence beacons we carry. Both the American and Israeli special forces have them. Pushing the transmit button, it sends out a code which a stand down signal, and identify us as friendly forces."

The men looked back and forth at each other.

"That's going to be tricky, Chief," Hicks said." I'd say the odds are against it, in this case."

J.D. continued.

"We also have to remove any technical equipment in the bunker that may be part of the Ultimate Sequential Numbering control box." J.D. looked around. "Do vou understand⁰"

He saw eleven nods in his direction, and noticed the urgency and danger involved in this mission was not lost on them.

Before J.D. could say more, a Naval Commander entered the room.

J.D. saluted him. "What is it, Sir?"

"Sorry to break in like this, Senior Chief," the commander responded, "but we just received flash traffic from Communications Center. You are to read it immediately."

J.D. looked at the decoded message alerting him to the presence of the Israelis and suddenly realized he had mislead his men. Not intentionally, of course. The mission had become far more complicated, now that the Israelis were headed for the same area as he and his squads were.

"Okay, gentlemen, get your gear and head for the hanger bay. Looks like we're going to have company. I'll explain on the way," J.D. said, picking up his briefing pack.

The team followed J.D. through the hatch and out into the hanger bay where the Ghost Shadow Squadron helos were being prepped for the mission. One by one, each squad entered their assigned helo which was then lifted to the flight deck by elevator and towed into launch position.

No sooner were all helos in place that the squawk box came alive.

“ATTENTION ALL SHIP’S PERSONNEL. CLEAR THE MAIN FLIGHT DECK AND PREPARE FOR LAUNCH.”

The first helo was in launch mode, the sequence began for mission departure.

“HELO... LAUNCH PAD ALPHA... BEGIN ROTATION...”

The blades of the first helo began to rotate. After the rotors had reached liftoff speed, the next order was given over the squawk.

-ALPHA PAD... LAUNCH HELO... LAUNCH HELO...

The first helo lifted off the flight deck, and headed out to sea.

After all helos were airborne, the squawk gave a final order.

“All HELOS AWAY FLIGHT DECK PERSONNEL STAND DOWN”

All four helos were on their way down range to their first Identification point. The operations phase of the mission was a ‘go’

Chapter 7

Flight into the Desert

The helos reached the coast of Libya in a little under an hour and head south after skirting Tobruk. The Ghost Shadow Squadron moved through the sky like flying carpets, gliding above the terrain below them. Each squad went through equipment checks and location maps. Every man had his assignment memorized as well as the alternative rescue and extraction plan.

Fifty-seven minutes later, the Alpha helo pilot alerted the first squad they were almost at the extraction point. J.D. nodded to his men, and, using hand signals, gestured that they were in landing mode. The aircraft descended quickly, touching down on the sandy surface near the enemy's perimeter. The squads scrambled out and headed south. Each helo lifted off after the squads disembarked and headed for the holding area to await recall to the extraction site.

The helos set down about I click (approximately .62 miles) from the target behind a natural sand dune terrain. J.D. 's Squad One turned on their night vision goggles , and moved carefully up the dune. At the top, they could see down into the bunker area. There didn't appear to be any signs of activity. J.D. hand signaled his squads to move to their designated positions.

The squads reported seeing no lights in the bunker area, no sentries on the perimeter outside the bunker. J.D. hand signaled the team to move to the north wall of the bunker compound, and enter through the gate area. Once the team entered the courtyard, they split up to find a door that would grant them access. Still there didn't appear to be anybody around. Squad 2 found an entry way and proceeded to the interior of the bunker structure. There was a narrow hallway leading about fifteen feet into the bunker. At the end of the hallway was a set of steps leading to a lower floor. Squads 1 and 2 moved slowly down the stairs which lead to an open room area. It was pitch black, as freshly poured tar. With their night vision goggles they could see several tables with computers perched and topography maps on the walls. A console on one side of the room contained equipment for satellite control. Whoever the occupants were, they appeared to have left in a hurry.

"Looks like we're to late, 'Chief', 'Swamp-Rat' said, scanning the reports on the table. "The hostiles have moved the 'package' already"

J.D. looked over the paperwork on the tables and alerted the Command Center on the Enterprise. He activated an encoded satellite communications radio known as a Sat Scrambler and started transmitting to the ship's command center.

"Falcon 1 , this is Station 5. Falcon 1 , this is station 5. (Station 5 indicates coded location of extraction team.)

"Falcon I Go ahead Station 5… Situation update…"

"…Station 5 empty, Falcon 1… The 'package' and 'joy box' still at large. Request Combat Control Center update mission compliance… Are there any changes in orders?."

"Roger, Station 5… We'll check and get back to you… end transmission…" A few minutes passed, and Eagle One responded to update the team.

"Falcon One to Station 5… You are to withdraw from current position, and direct mission to the north, and continue to track 'package'… Try and locate 'package' and 'joy box' and complete extraction. Neutralize current position… Out…"

"Understood, Falcon One We're on our way… Station 5… Out…" J.D. turned to his squads.

"Let's go, guys. Falcon One wants us to continue tracking the 'package' and try again," J.D. said securing the Sat Scrambler back into the side pack.

The squads placed high explosive charges on the load bearing areas of the bunker, set the timers for five minutes, and left the bunker like gazelles being chased by lions.

J.D. was somewhat surprised that Command (Falcon One) requested pursuit.

He knew how urgent it was to recover the 'package' , but Command usually had a Plan B, which involved additional air support. With four stealth helos, it was still possible to overtake and engage the hostiles.

J.D. signaled the helos, and in two minutes, the Spec-Ops were on board and lifted off the dessert floor. The pilots had been advised by Eagle Eye as to the new heading.

Chapter 8

Chase Across the Desert

J.D. gazed at the map, running several scenarios' in his mind, in case they were able to intercept the 'package'.

Suddenly the voice of the pilot of Alpha helo, came over the headsets.

"All squads, Code Red... Hostile ground activity five clicks down range... Radar indicates heavy ground fire and explosions... All helos form on me and prepare to engage... Ground squads prepare to disembark on touch-down..."

All four squads prepared for landing, and a ground assault. J.D. 's squad would be the first in, He slammed a fully loaded ammo clip into his assault rifle and prepared to disembark on landing.

The helos entered the hot landing zone, firing its 20 mm mini-guns as several rocket propelled grenades whizzed past them. Alpha helo swept in, hovered for a few seconds and landed. J.D. and Squad 1 jumped out of the helo, weapons blazing, and Alpha helo did a rapid lift-off.

Helos Bravo, Charlie, and Delta followed Alpha helo in, activating their 20 mm guns as they were hovering to land, dropping the other three squads, and then rapid lift-off.

Primary hostile fire was coming from a disabled tank.

J.D., 'Swamp-Rat' and 'Bagger' positioned themselves in a triangular formation in the dunes and were taking heavy fire as they did so. Several incoming rounds barely missed hitting 'Bagger'.

"I've had just about enough of this!" Bagger' yelled to J.D. "J.D.... Toss me a Laws rocket!"

J.D. removed the rocket from his equipment bag and tossed it to 'Bagger' o He picked it up, pulled the holding pin for the front and rear tube protectors, and positioned himself facing the tank. He placed it on his shoulder, aimed, and pulled the trigger. Flames flew from the rear of the tube as the rocket head for the tank. Two seconds later, the tank exploded into a fireball and covered the surrounding area with hot pieces of flying metal, neutralizing all the hostiles around it.

Squads 2, 3, and 4 had flanked Squad 1 and moved to more strategic positions to repel possible counter attack fire.

"Squad I ... Lets roll!" yelled J.D. The other squads moved to the right and left of the explosion area, littered with bodies, weapons, and burning debris. There, they encountered more incoming fire from one of the dunes.

'Hoops' was the best sniper on J.D.'s team.

"'Hoops'," yelled J.D., "That guy up on that dune has us pinned down with machine gun fire. Can you get to those palm trees to the right of that dune and 'punch his ticket'?"

'Hoops' reached in his bag of weapons, pulled out what he called 'the Bushmaster', a special sniper rifle, pieced it together, and signaled J.D. to give him cover fire until he reached the palm trees.

Using his powerful legs, 'Hoops' ran the gauntlet as fast as he could, zigging and zagging, and finally jumping into the clump of palm trees. Sand was flying from everywhere around his path from bullets hitting the sand trying to bring him down.

"'Doc', you and 'Preacher' lay down suppression fire for about 10 seconds, then stop." 'Hoops' yelled. Then, 'Hoops' said under his breath, "When our 'friend' pops his head up, 'BLAM!'... problem solved."

One minute later, the distinctive sound of the 'Bushmaster' caused the sounds coming from the targeted dune to go silent. The squads moved into the combat zone.

The squads swept the area, which looked like a campsite, but found no signs of hostiles. Based on the amount of weapons, field equipment, and mess kits, and boot prints, there were at least seven to ten men. 'Hoops' walked up the dune behind the camp, and called to J.D.

"Chief You better come look at this."

J.D. Walked up to where 'Hoops was standing, and looked down. There, on the other side of the dune lay four decapitated bodies.

"These guys are "Israelis, J.D. said. "Most likely commandos. Probably captured at some point and brought along, and were executed here… The hostiles didn't want any excess baggage slowing them down…"

The SAT Phone beeped and J.D. pulled it from his side pack.

"Fledglings, this is Eagle Eye… Stand by for incoming Flash Traffic… 'Eagle Eye was the airborne early warning aircraft that monitored the operation from high altitude.

"Six boogies inbound in HALO formation Three high, three low." (3 aircraft incoming high altitude, 3 aircraft incoming at low altitude). "Probably Libyan fighter aircraft… "After a few seconds delay, further information continued.

"Two more unknown aircraft just showed up on our radar, flying at Mach 0.9 just south of the HALO group…

J.D. Looked over at 'Hoops".

"Those last two gotta' be Israeli aircraft. From the speed, I'd say they were F-B2 Hummingbirds, Israelis new interceptors…"

J.D. and 'Hoops descended back down the dune heading for the helos. They could hear the incoming aircraft.

The SAT Phone beeped and J.D. once again pulled it from its pack.

"Fledglings…" Eagle Eye transmitted, "Those two new aircraft have split off and are engaging the HALO aircraft. They just fired missiles at them… The missiles are on target and overtaking the hostiles …Wax two high (2 aircraft kills)… Wax two low (2 more aircraft kills)…"

The sky lit up as one of the hostile low flying hostile aircraft was hit by a Hawk-Hunter Israeli missile causing the hostile aircraft to spiral to the ground. It crashed 70 feet from the Alpha Helo, sending a fireball and molten pieces of debris in all directions.

J.D. was sliding down a dune when a piece of metal tore through his flak jacket, partially penetrating it and opening a gash in his chest. Another piece of metal ripped open a four-inch long gash in his left leg. J.D. dropped to the ground and grabbed his wounded leg.

"'Chiefs' hit! ... "Chief's' Hit!" 'Hoops' yelled.

'Doc' scrambled over to J.D. and began dressing his wounds. As he removed his flak jacket, the SAT Phone beeped again. It was the radio operator from the AWAC's aircraft.

"Fledglings This is Eagle Eye Remaining hostile aircraft have changed course, and are heading north toward Tobruk. Unknown pursuit aircraft have veered off and are heading out towards the Mediterranean Sea..."

'Doc' took the phone from J.D.'s hand and returned response.

"Eagle Eye 'Chief's' been hit in the chest and left leg. His chest wound appears superficial, and I'll have to throw a couple of stitches in his leg wound. He'll be all right until we get back to Falcon's Nest. Any change in mission status?" 'Doc asked.

"Fledglings This is Eagle One. Are you still capable of continuing the mission?" came the response.

"We still have the whole team," replied 'Doc'. "We'll just change 'Chiefs' status to 'observer'!

J.D. looked up giving 'Doc' a slight sneer.

'Hoops' and 'Bagger helped J.D. over to Alpha helo and loaded him on board.

The Alpha helo pilot's voice sounded from the intercom.

"Alpha helo to squadron group Lift-off... Lift-off.... Lift-off... Follow my lead... Heading 0-9-0 azimuth."

Alpha helo headed on the new course and the other helos followed in a split tangent formation.

Again, Flash Traffic came over the SAT Phone.

"Eagle Eye to Fledglings. Topography mapping showing two helos on the ground with a three truck convoy 50 miles north of your current position... Contrast radar shows helos are Ta-50 Black Sharks military helos they are definitely Russian Do you copy, Fledglings?..."

"Hoops' looked over at J.D. "What do we do now, 'Chief'?

J-D. picked up the SAT Phone and responded.

"Eagle Eye, advise Falcon One. Ask Command if we are still to pursue and engage."

Eagle Eye notified Falcon One of the situation.

There was a pregnant pause as the CCC decided what course of action the United States was going to take. Suddenly Russia and the United States had attack helos inside the territory of a sovereign nation, Egypt. Neither of the superpowers were supposed to be there. If the United States chose to engage the Russian helos. the incident would escalate and bring into play additional forces and turn the area into a powder keg.

"Fledglings, this is Falcon One... DO NOT, repeat, DO NOT engage the Black Shark helos... Withdraw to a secure position and hold... Eagle Eye will contact you when the Russians depart the area..."

The Ghost Shadow Squadron dropped down closer to the terrain and looked for a secure site. Once they established a site, they touched down but maintained rotor rotation for immediate lift-off if necessary. Five minutes passed, and the SAT phone beeped. It was Eagle Eye.

"Fledglings... firefight in progress at the convoy site Black Sharks helos involved ... investigate at once..."

"Roger, Eagle Eye... We're on our way," J.D. responded.

The Ghost Shadow Squadron lifted off and headed to the battle area.

Alpha helo reached the area first and circled. Three armored vehicles below were on fire, flames of red and orange licking the sky. Bodies were scattered all around the trucks in defensive positions. The truck convoy had been completely destroyed.

Alpha helo landed about fifty yards from the convoy, and Squad I proceeded to the firefight zone. Helos Bravo, Charlie, and Delta remained circling the perimeter to ensure safety of the ground team.

Carefully, J.D. and his men approached the armored vehicles. Upon the inspection of the scene, Squad 1 found evidence of high explosive munitions used on the convoy, and evidence of 20 mm mini-gun strafing. The attack was definitely the work of the Ka50 Black Shark helos.

No one was left alive and Professor Goldschmidt was nowhere to be found. "Hoops walked around the vehicles, inspected their armament, and then examined the firearms the shooters had used. He walked back over to J.D. looking a little puzzled.

"I just realized something, 'Chief,'" 'Hoops' said. "The first group of hostiles at the bunker were in desert clothing and had standard weapons. They were part of the Red Scorpion Brigade, but this group has camo clothing and they're carrying heavy weaponry. This looks like the work of mercenary soldiers, probably independent contractors from South Africa."

J.D. surveyed the situation.

"Seems like everybody is after the same 'package'," he said. "What I'd like to know is how all these people knew about this. Let's get back to the helos and radio Falcon's Nest on what we found," J.D. shouldered his weapon and took the Sat Phone out of its carrier. Once the squad was back on the helo, J.D. called Falcon's Nest.

"Fledglings, Station 5, to Falcon's Nest with Flash Traffic..." J.D. spoke into the microphone on the SAT Phone. "Do you copy, Falcon's Nest?"

"This is Falcon's Nest," came the reply, "Ready to copy."

J.D. began his report.

"It appears that mercenaries hit the Red Scorpion Brigade just north of the bunker, and continued north after grabbing the 'package' and the Black Sharks took THEM out and grabbed the 'package'. We're currently going back to the Mediterranean on the original azimuth. Over."

"Falcon's Nest, additional Flash Traffic. A Russian battle group has just entered the Mediterranean Sea... All helos return to base...0ver and out."

Communications ended and the Ghost Shadow Squadron was on its way back to the carrier.

Chapter 9

Two days Prior to These Events...

Chris Logan decided to take a personal day, not for any particular reason, other than getting his head together. He needed time alone to contemplate his life, where he was headed. He drove out to the park next to the Conservatory, parked his car. and began walking down the concrete walk. Chris liked this particular area because halfway down and to the left there was a slight incline that lead to a small bridge that lead to a small bridge between two elm trees. He remembered all the times he spent with Elise in Park Vue while stationed in the Air Force. What he remembered most, though, was the last time they spoke: when he told her he was leaving on a top-secret mission for a year. That they couldn't see each other or communicate the entire time. Every other memory associated with the rustic wooden bridge carried happiness. That one, though? It was bitter sweet.

Chris sat down on a park bench and looked toward the bridge, reminiscing. He never heard the steps from behind until a stranger appeared.

"Good morning, my son." the man said.

Chris looked up into his face. He saw a man with a dark beard, a little over six feet tall, with steel blue eyes, and wearing a black hat like the rest of his clothing. That's when Chris saw it, the tiny silver crucifix hanging from the stranger's neck. Looking further down his torso, Chris noticed he had a Bible in his right hand. He appeared to be a priest.

"I'm sorry, Father, I didn't hear you," Chris. He stood and faced he man.

"Oh, that's quite all right," replied the priest, "Please. Sit.

Both men sat down on the bench and exchanged small talk for a few minutes. The man introduced himself as Father Joseph Ignatius. A Professor of Theology at the Holy Fathers University across the city.

"Are you Catholic?" the priest asked.

"No, Father," replied Chris, "Protestant."

"Do you read the Bible?" the priest continued.

"Yes. Father. but not as often as I should."

"Do you have any favorite books in the Bible, in the Old or the New Testaments?"

Chris hesitated before answering.

- 'I like reading the Palms in the Old Testament, and Ephesians in the New Testament... I often go to the one passage from Ephesians about putting on the full armor of God... That always seems to lift me up when I need it the most." The priest looked away from Chris, seeming to peer into the distance.

"My favorite books are Proverbs, from the Old Testament , because of the wisdom and foresight; and my favorite books of the New testament are Matthew, Mark, Luke, and John..."

He slowly turned his head back towards Chris. Chris felt like he had been hit with a thunderbolt as he gazed into the priest's eyes! It had been at least twenty years since he had heard those names emphasized like that. The last time was in a briefing before he left the Four Apostles Project. What was going on? Why was the project being brought up now? The priest slowly rose from the bench.

"I have a class on those four books at 1 p.m. today at the Holy Fathers University... It would be in your best interest to be there... Benson Hall, Room 107... You really should attend the session..." The priest walked away, in the direction of the Conservatory.

Chris sat there dumbfounded. The project was completed by the beginning of the 70's, and he was sure the laser platforms were in orbit by now. Why was there a problem now in 2008? Did something breakdown? Were the platforms in a decaying orbit? It could be anything.

He Stood up and looked toward the conservatory. The priest was gone! Chris hurried back to his car.

Chapter 10

Complicated Operations

Chris drove into the lower level of the university parking lot and found a parking space close to Benson Hall. It was 12:50 p.m. He went into the building and walked down the stairs, then proceeded down the corridor until he came to Room 107. Ihe door was slightly ajar. Chris slowly turned the door handle and went inside. At the front right comer stood three men, Father Ignatius and two others dressed in monk's garb.

"Chris, Glad you could make it," Father Ignatius said gesturing Chris over with his hand. "There are a couple of people I would like you to meet."

Chris walked over hesitantly, not knowing what to expect. The man who called himself Father Ignatius was in reality John Percival, National Security Agency. The monks introduced themselves as Hank Sherman, CIA, and Mitchell Forrestal, FBI.

"Relax, Chris," Percival said, "You're here for an update briefing on the Four Apostles Project. Here's the problem: Two nights ago professor Goldschmidt was kidnapped from his laser laboratory. We believe that a radical off-shoot group faction from the Middle East, the Red Scorpion Brigade, is responsible. They killed four guards at the facility to get to Goldschmidt. They also took an Ultimate Number Sequencing Unit — 1. If they obtain the new activating code from Goldschmidt by using truth serum or the information on his laptop, this dangerous group can take control of the laser platforms."

"Is there any kind of self-destruct mechanism in the sequencing unit we can utilize to disable it so the codes won't work?" asked Forrestal.

"In the original prototype," Chris explained, "we placed a small explosive charge inside that had to be activated by a two-person key system. If they have Goldschmidt, they also have one of the keys. Without the other key, which is locked in an iron safe in the Command Center, there is no way to disable it. With no way to disable the sequencer, they can task the satellites and aim those lasers on any target they wish."

The four men sat down at a table in the front of the room and Percival opened a packet identical to the one Chris saw when he was working on the tasking system for the laser platforms.

"The basic problem is to get to the aiming and firing mechanism and reroute the signal to the null analyzer to shut the lasers down." Chris began.

"In this particular system, there are modules set up to complete specific tasks. Each module is a small plug-in electronics board that carries electronic data to and from the main computer 'mother board'. If I can get to the original schematics, I might be able to locate a 'backdoor' into the aiming and firing mechanism."

Percival opened his briefcase and produced current schematics of the platforms guidance, aiming, and firing system, spreading them out on the table.

"The whole concept of the firing mechanism is based on applying the right signal through what is called an 'engram', which is an altered human gene structure merged with artificial intelligence." Chris explained.

"I helped trouble-shoot this particular module when I worked on the project in 1970." Chris said. "These plans were classified so top-secret because back then, It was a quantum leap in laser operations when it came to using human genetic structures with artificial intelligence on printed circuit boards."

Percival's mind was swirling with the idea of human and artificial intelligence merging to operate a machine. He spoke up.

"Are you saying that our scientists got this to work, and was almost immediately turned into weapon usage?" He began. "Our scientists have developed not only artificial intelligence, but these 'engrams' could be tasked to make decisions also?"

"Professor Goldschmidt did the initial work on the process and accomplished far more than he intended." Chris replied.

Chris turned his head to Percival. "That's right, Mr. Percival, and that was just the beginning. In my opinion, I believe we have advanced the use of these units to far greater uses, and will eventually be our downfall."

Chris scanned the schematics to try and figure where to start.

"According to what I'm looking at on these schematics, additional electronic by-pass gates were added to the circuitry to accommodate the new algorithm. The sequence is read here," as he pointed to a module on the schematic, "then. sent to the ' 'engram' transposer, where the coding is reversed and re-sequenced here. Using his left hand and pointed to another spot on the modular schematic. "Then, the signal is sent to the final code area. The new algorithm controls these gates with an additional feedback mechanism."

Chris looked up from the table.

"This is a more complicated process than the original design, Chris said. "It makes it harder to access the circuitry on the platforms and activate the lasers, if you don't know what you are doing."

Percival looked worried. "Our main concern is this: Is there a way we can insert a by-pass that would allow us to filter the signal out and manipulate the algorithm so the final sequence is blocked, by using a 'back door' technique you mentioned Chris?"

Chris looked down toward the schematics again.

"It's been years since I worked on the project. I'd have to meet with the engineers that help design this system, particularly the engineers that worked on the 'engram' module. With the new algorithm, there may be some data that has been re-routed or has feedback to other areas. I won't know until I talk with them"

"I guess the course is clear," remarked Percival. He turned and looked at Chris.

"I'11 see to it that you will be released from your normal job duties, and you can come with us to Washington D.C. "Your wife and children will be taken to a safe house for the time being."

With that, the briefing seemed to be adjourned, as the four men started moving toward the door. This was going way too fast for Chris.

Chris stopped as they approached the door.

"Whoa! Wait a minute, you guys," Chris exclaimed. "My family knows nothing about this project or what part I played in it. Why are you bringing them into it?

Percival abruptly stopped and turned to Chris.

"We have reason to believe that you and your family are being watched by the very people who were watching you twenty years ago. If they have no success with Goldschmidt or his computer, guess who is next on the list. Our enemies know how closely you worked with the new technology that helped produce these weapons. Trust me, they will have no qualms about using your family as leverage with you. Your family will either be threatened with violence or will be kidnapped and have body parts sent to you; they will send videos with them doing things to your family, believe me, you wouldn't want to watch. Do you understand NOW, Chris?!" Percival was almost yelling.

This was like a punch in the face to Chris. His family was his life. The very thought of them suffering because of his involvement in this mess turned his stomach. He kicked a chair across the room before he exited.

The four men headed out of Benson Hall, on to the Commons area, and down the steps to their vehicles. Chris walked next to Percival.

"Chris," Percival said, "I'll have someone come over and pick up your car. You come to the airport with me. Don't worry about clothes or anything else. We have everything you need on the plane. Anything else we can get in D.C."

Percival made several cell phone calls from the NSA vehicle on the way to the airport to set up the scenarios to explain Chris's and his wife, Jessie's absence from the respective jobs. His one call was to NSA security to provide protection for Chris's children. The last call Percival made went directly to Langley, Virginia, home of the CIA.

"I need to know what's going on RIGHT NOW with this Four Apostles project." Percival said to the agent on the other end of the line.

"Yes, sir!" Came the response. "Tie in to SALVO LINE 7."

He opened his lap-top computer and proceeded to enter the required code.

A face appeared on the screen of the computer once the code cleared.

"A whole lot of things are going on, John," The non-descript man said. "The Russians have moved a battle group consisting of two heavy cruisers, an aircraft carrier, three destroyers — one a guided missile destroyer — and the usual support surface craft. We are assuming at least two, if not three, Type 0-9-1 Han class fast attack nuclear submarines will be making their way to join the battle group. The battle group left Vladivostok yesterday and is moving south at flank speed. Our guess is that they're headed for the Mediterranean Sea.

The man on the screen continued with his report.

"Libya has put its air force on alert and activated its surface-to-air missile sites. Israel has placed the entire Israeli Defense force on full alert, and our satellites show several Israeli airbases air bases are preparing for an air strike. Most of the aircraft appear to be their new fighter-bomber aircraft, the FB-2 Hummingbird, and they're carrying the Hawk-Hunter missiles."

"A lot of terrorist chatter is coming out of Syria and Lebanon. Most of it is being decoded now. But it seems to indicate that Professor Goldschmidt is no longer in their hands. Another military group grabbed him in the Libyan desert. We are monitoring every development as it is happening in real time, and the President has raised the alert status to DEFCON 4.

The speaker on the computer screen seemed to be receiving updates faster than he could read them.

The U.S.S. Enterprise battle group is currently in the Mediterranean Sea, headed East. Two sea Wolf class fast attack nuclear submarines are joining the battle group along with a Virginia class nuclear submarine."

"Overall, there will be two major power battle groups running parallel to each other in the Mediterranean. This situation can get out of hand very quickly with that much power in one area".

At this point, Percival was running all possible scenarios through his head. He had to get Chris to Washington, to the laser lab outside the capital, if they had any hope of keeping the four laser satellites from falling into hostile hands.

We're headed to the airport," Percival said to the person on the other side of the computer screen. "Tell the Joint Chiefs I'll meet them in the Rapid Response Room in three hours. Also, tell them Chris Logan is with me and his family is in protective custody."

"Yes, sir," came the response and the transmission was terminated.

Percival closed the his laptop sighing in frustration.

The drive to the airport took thirty minutes, then another five minute drive to the Air National Guard side of the airstrip. A Gulfstream military jet awaited them. The pilot opened the front passenger door of the car as it stopped thirty feet from the jet.

"Wheels up in five minutes. gentlemen. Please board the aircraft and strap in."

Chapter 11

Back Channel

The Gulfstream jet touched down and hour and thirty-six minutes later, landing on a little secluded and barely known airstrip outside of Washington D.C. Percival had continued to update all current information on Operation Blue Light throughout the flight. After deplaning, an Air Force Colonel drove them to the White House. Four Marines escorted Chris and John to the Rapid Response Room. The Military Chiefs of Staff were gathered around one side of the table and Jack Logan was sitting on the opposite side. Percival and Chris took their place next to Jack.

Armed Services Chief of Staff General Rhodes spoke first.

"It looks as if this operation can go critical in a relatively short time. The Red Scorpion Brigade was supposedly responsible for kidnapping Professor Goldschmidt. Now, we're hearing they don't have him. And if they don't have him, who does?"

Percival looked up from the intelligence reports he had been studying.

"We've received additional information from the Mediterranean battle group, General Rhodes," Percival said as he sifted through the reports in front of him.

"Operation Blue Light was to withdraw from the area. The Red Scorpion Brigade had Goldschmidt at the bunker. Their intelligence network informed them that our contingency group was headed in their direction and to move the professor to avoid capture. In the process, they encountered a group of mercenaries, and a firefight ensued. The Red Scorpion Brigade fighters were all killed, and the mercenaries made off with the professor. Then, they were attacked by Russian Ka50 Black Shark helicopters and we now assume the Russians have him."

"If the Russians have him, why are they sending a battle group into the Mediterranean?" asked Admiral McNay, the Naval Chief of Operations. If they've already captured Goldschmidt, I'm sure they'll try and smuggle him out of Libya. They certainly wouldn't need a whole battle group for that."

Percival turned and looked at Ja ck.

"The Russian battle group may be a diversion for something else... But what?" Jack asked, seemingly to himself.

Chris looked down at the images on the table monitors. The images were in real time, and Chris noticed something in an isolated area outside Tobruk. Two Ka50 Black Shark helicopters were sitting on the ground with no heat radiating from the jet exhaust on the aircraft.

Jack and General Rhodes noticed them too. Why were they sifting there cold when they could be used to withdraw to the Russian battle group, once it reached the area?

General Rhodes spoke up.

"This is some kind of ruse," the general remarked. "They've GOT to know that if they attempt to fly out to the ships, that our fast attack subs will take them out with Scout missiles. They would be shot down before they could get to the Russian battle group."

As everyone in the room was trying to decide what the Russians were going to do, and what the United States response was going to be, Jack noticed a small green light was flashing in the bottom of his laptop computer screen. He touched the F 12 key, and the light disappeared. He slowly stood up from the table. He pushed his chair back and started to walk away from the conference table.

"Where are you going?" asked Percival.

Jack just kept walking.

"I'm going to the Pentagon to look at the regional maps for that part of the Mediterranean. There may be something we're overlooking." With that, he exited the room and headed down the corridor. Halfway down the corridor, Jack entered a restroom, and locked the door. He knew he a short time to do what he had to do.

He sat down on the seat of the commode, opened his laptop and pushed the F 12 key.

Within seconds the screen lit up and an encrypted code appeared at the top left side. Jack typed in a code below the first one, and the channel opened for dialog. A green text appeared out of nowhere on the screen, as if a ghost were typing it.

Jack peered at the message closely. The substance of the dialog was Operation Blue Light.

The Russian at the other end of the computer link used the code initials BC (Bear Claw) Jack used the code initials WW (West Wind).

BC: 'The U.S. battle group has drawn the wrong conclusion for the Russian presence in the Mediterranean. All is not as it seems. They do not have Professor Goldschmidt. They are on another mission.' It read.

Jack looked at the message, puzzled, and began typing a reply.

WW: 'Do not understand... Why so much show of force if they do not have the professor?'

BC: 'Person who now has Professor Goldschmidt is known as Anatoly Vertof, a Russian criminal. Two days ago, he and four of his gang stole two Ka-50 Black Shark helicopters and one troop carrier helicopter from one of our air bases.

The air defense system radar lost them when they went into stealth mode.'

Jack now knew who had the professor, but he still didn 't know why.

BC continued the message.

BC: Vertof 's intel alerted him to the fact that the Red Scorpion Brigade was going to kidnap Goldschmidt to obtain the tasking algorithm and the UNSU-I for the Four Apostle Satellites to blackmail the United States and Israel into concessions on the Sinai and Palestine, and the withdrawal of all American personnel from the area. Vertof decided he would wait until the Red Scorpion Brigade kidnapped him and brought him to Libya before his group He would kidnap the professor from them and holding him for the highest bidder. Vertof failed to realize that South African mercenaries were aware of the kidnapping, and had the same plan as he had. The Ka-50 Black Shark helicopters had more armament than the mercenaries had, so it was no problem neutralizing their forces.'

Jack was still trying to figure out the Russian power bid in the Mediterranean. He replied to BC.

WW:' What is the reason the Russian battle group is in the Mediterranean then?'

BC: 'The Russians are in the Mediterranean to capture Vertof and return him to Russia for prosecution of crimes against the state. He has a computer with him that has all his illegal contacts, bank accounts, corrupt Russian official's names and security information about the government. He is an extreme liability to the government infrastructure, and the information on that computer can, if released, cause the collapse of the Russian socioeconomic system, and fall of the current government and plunge the country into chaos.

Jack questioned again as to what was happening on the Russian side. WW: 'Does Russia plan to communicate these details to the United States?'

BC: 'No… Not at this time. Their fleet is to divert attention away from covert ops on Libyan soil. But their real mission has not been divulged yet. It is apparently something that Russia has been planning for some time, but had to wait until an opportunity presented itself. If, in the meantime, they acquire the professor, I doubt they will return him to the United States or Israel.

Suddenly there was a knock on the bathroom door. Jack flipped his laptop closed, which automatically cut the connection to his backchannel to Russia.

"Jack, it's John Percival. Are you all right in there? You didn't show up at the entrance, and I thought you had gotten sick or something."

"I'm Okay." Replied Jack, "Just a bit of gastrointestinal flair-up. I'll be out in a couple of minutes."

"All right" Percival said as he walked away." I'll tell the Marine guards at the door you'll be along in a few minutes."

That was close! close! Jack had established a back channel to the Kremlin when he was appointed Middle East Chief of Operations for the CIA. He and his contact would work together to defuse volatile situations that could lead to an all out nuclear confrontation. No one knew that this type of communications existed between the two super powers.

Jack gathered his briefcase and computer together and left the restroom and headed for the front door. The Marine guard signed him out. He went to his car and headed to the Pentagon.

"How are we going to handle this without getting into a shooting scenario? Jack thought to himself. 'And what about the Israeli response?

Chapter 12

Israeli Response

While the super powers were posturing in the Mediterranean, Israel 's Israeli Defense Forces generals and their National Security Council were meeting in Tel Aviv's equivalent the White House Rapid Response Room. Prime Minister Cohen looked the long table in front of him. The 'Hawks' and the 'Doves were huddling in their respective positions. Some plan of action to return Professor Goldschmidt safely to Israeli shores had to be developed. The Prime Minister called the session to order.

"Gentlemen... Gentlemen. Please be seated so we can address this situation and decide a proper response."

"As you know, our top physicist was kidnapped from his laboratory in the United States forty-eight hours ago. Everything indicates that the Red Scorpion Brigade was responsible. They are currently headed for the Middle East. We are not sure where he is to be taken, but probably Palestine. There they plan to use his knowledge of the Four Apostles defense system to gain control of the four satellites and re-task them to strike Israeli territory. If this occurs, we will be helpless to defend ourselves and we will have to concede to whatever demands are placed before us."

IDF Air Force General Ben-Suri spoke up.

"Mr. Prime Minister, we obviously have no choice in this situation... We must obtain the release of Professor Goldschmidt. Our intelligence places him in a bunker 430 kilometers south of Tobruk. If we fail to extract him at that point, we must continue the hunt until we do find him. He is far too valuable to be captured. If extraction fails, do we have permission for a sanction?"

Serious faces from both sides of the table looked up toward the Prime Minister. Everyone at the table knew what that meant… If all other attempts failed, Professor Goldschmidt would have to be sacrificed. No one wanted that.

IDF Army Chief of Staff was second to speak up.

"Our IDF Army has commandos in the general area. Their intel puts the professor at that bunker in the desert. They have already headed towards the objective and will notify us as soon as they take the objective."

Prime Minister Cohen rose from his seat to issue orders.

"I want four FB-2's airborne and on alert immediately, so we can respond immediately if the situation calls for it. Also, two airborne refueling aircraft will be launched to be on standby alert in case our fighters need to be airborne longer than anticipated. Our aircraft will be in international airspace north of Tobruk. I expect the United States Military will enter into this situation at some point, if they haven't done so already. Both our countries have our missions, so the situation can become very complicated very quickly."

The Council continued discussing the preparations for the mission, and the defenses necessary for homeland security as well.

The Israeli Command and Control Center issued orders for the military mission to extract Professor Goldschmidt. Army ground forces were put on high alert and the four FB-2's and the two refueling aircraft eased into take-off position on the tarmac.

The final decision to commit was in the hands of the Prime Minister. The Prime Minister picked up his phone and called the air base tower. "Launch alert aircraft!" Israeli response to the threat was set in motion.

Chapter 13

Anatoly Vertof

Six hundred and thirty-four miles away south east from Tel Aviv, Anatoly Vertof landed his twin engine Beechcraft aircraft four miles south of Tobruk. Vertof , a tall, stocky man in his early forties, with a black beard and dark brown eyes brown eyes and dressed in military camos and camo hat, stepped out of the aircraft, and jumped to the ground. As he surveyed the surrounding terrain, two Black Shark helicopters and a helicopter troop carrier landed about one hundred feet away. Fifty men were on board the troop carrier, some were mercenaries and some were former Russian commandos. Best of all, Vertof had Goldschmidt. The good professor had been transported on the troop carrier with the commandos. Vertof gave an evil chuckle as he walked toward the helicopters, at how well his plan was working.

Five trucks were obtained from the village, and Vertof proceeded north towards Tobruk with his convoy. During his absence, ten commandoes were left behind to protect the villagers and to make sure the mercenaries didn't decide to take off with his aircraft.

When they reached a split in the road, they took a right and drove ten minutes more, as the road turned into a narrow dirt lane that lead them into a large palm tree grove. There, several small block buildings sat in total silence. They appeared to be abandoned. The convoy rolled to a stop at the last building they came to.

Vertof and six of his commandos stealthily entered the building, descend a stairway fifteen feet under the building. They emerged underground in a well illuminated room twice the area of the floor above them. Two commandos took Goldschmidt to the far side of the room where they bound his hands and feet to a sturdy metal chair.

Electronic devices and computer monitors hung from the walls. On the east side of the room, there was a control console and command station sitting on a table. Vertof settled into a chair there, put the headpiece on, and activated a series of switches to give him full use of the control panel and computer.

He set the encryption codes and passwords of the system software in order to begin communications, They typed in a coded sequence of alpha-numeric characters, which appeared in the upper left corner of the monitor screen. About ten seconds later, his computer was locked into another system outside of Moscow.

A message began to appear on the monitor screen. The message was from someone using the code name 'Red Palace' and was being sent to Vertof's code name, 'Artic Wolf.

'Red Palace': 'Have you picked up the package?'

'Artic Wolf (reply): 'The package is with us… Had to neutralize another customer looking for the same package… Expect the United States to try to obtain package also.'

'Red Palace': Sources have informed me that there are four 'special' helicopters out hunting already, code name the Ghost Shadow Squadron… The Russian Northern Fleet is in the mix too. They are headed into the area also. We will proceed with the bidding for the 'package' once you have cleared your present location.

'Artic Wolf': 'We are just outside the staging area. The bunker is fully operationally ready. Once the battle groups engage, and confusion takes over, we will make our escape by the method we agreed upon''

'Red Palace': 'Ensure that we receive, intact, what we sent you for. End of transmission.'

Vertof switched frequencies for the computer transmitter, and contacted his commandos.

"'Artic Wolf" to 'Wolf Cubs' do you read?

There was a brief pause, then then a squawk came across the airwaves. The 'Wolf Cubs' were checking in.

"Is the village still secure, and are there any signs of activity from anyone?" Vertof asked?

"Everything is quiet here," replied 'Cub 1'. "How soon do you want the helos ready to go?"

"I'm waiting for the go code from 'Red Palace'," Vertof answered. "As soon as the code is transmitted, I'll let you know and you can bring all of the helos to my present position. I'll brief you when you arrive.'

"Understood. 'Cub I' out."

Chapter 14

Standoff in the Mediterranean

Eight hours after the American battle group passed through the Straits of Gibraltar, the Russian battle group followed. Just as their counterparts had done earlier, The Russian battle group headed for the center of the Levantine Basin, at the Turkish side of the sea. However, unbeknownst to the Russians, re-tasked American satellites were recording the Russian positions.

Two of the three Russian nuclear submarines were now on station at one thousand yards from the battle group. They kept their sonar active to insure no other submarines were in the area. Soon the third nuclear submarine arrived, was properly identified, and the Russian battle group was complete.

Back in Washington, Jack was in the Ready Response Room with the President, the Military Chiefs of Staff, the Secretary of Defense, The Secretary of State, and various other strategists.

"What now?' asked the Secretary of Defense Ronald Stafford.

The President furrowed his eyebrows and looked down to a computer that was tracking real time events and progress from the satellite stations.

"Unless I miss my guess," President Steele replied, "The Russians will parallel their course with our battle group. They know that any attempt they make to extract Goldschmidt will be met with force."

The President turned and looked at Admiral Charles Pruist, Chief of Naval Operations in the Mediterranean, who was sitting across from him.

"Any suggestions, Admiral Pruist?" said the President.

The admiral picked up the ball and ran with it.

"First of all, I think that we should contact the Russians and let them know what OUR interest is in this. Let them know that we will keep a sufficient distance between the battle groups, so to avoid a confrontation."

"Second, we augment our satellites with the AWAC's and put four Ready Alert F-14's in the air. Have a refueling aircraft in the air also, in case we need to keep our fighters in the air for an extended period of time. This is a bit of 'saber-rattling', but it should give the Russians something to think about."

"Third, continue surveillance on the area south of Tobruk, where the professor was last known to be. I don't know how they intend to get him out, but I'm sure they'll try some sort of diversion tactic."

"Mr. President," continued the admiral, "Do we have permission to fire on the Russians, if provoked?"

The President stared back down at the table, and quietly gave the order. "You will fire only if fired upon. Is that quite clear?" asked the President.

"Yes, Mr. President. only if fired upon," repeated Admiral Pruist.

Jack swung his chair around and addressed Admiral Pruist.

"Admiral, would we be able to continue Operation Blue Light? The Ghost Shadow Squadron is back on the Enterprise, but can be put on Ready Alert to assist with whatever action is taken on the ground. With any luck, we might be able to do a 'Hail Mary' and extract the professor before they knew what hit them.'

Admiral Pruist looked down at the map of the Tobruk area and had several other admirals and generals give their opinions on Jack's proposal. After five minutes passed, Admiral Pruist walked over to Jack.

"Jack, I want you to contact your brother and see what he thinks. If anyone can pull it off, J.D. and his Spec-Ops team can." I want him to call me after he accesses the situation."

Jack gave a half smile. He knew he'd get his brother back in the game.

"Yes, sir," Jack responded. "I'll call the Enterprise immediately."

The Enterprise was on full alert when the ship's intercom announced:

ATTENTION ON DECK… NOW HEAR THIS… NOW HEAR THIS… BLUE LIGHT GROUP REPORT TO THE READY ROOM… BLUE LIGHT GROUP REPORT TO THE READY ROOM…'

J.D. returned from Sick Bay and headed for the Ready Room. Apparently, there was going to be more to this operation than originally intended. As he stepped across the bulkhead to enter the compartment, 'Bagger' pulled him aside and handed him the Sat phone.

"Your brother's on the line", 'Chief' "Says he needs to talk to you."

"Yeah, Jack… What's in the wind?" J.D. asked after taking the receiver.

"I just had a pow-wow with the Chief of Naval Operations on the Mediterranean area, along with some other top brass, and they seem to think that Operation Blue Light is still viable, and want you to continue the mission if you feel we have a chance for the extraction. They want you to go back in and do what you need to do to solve this problem." Jack explained.

J.D. thought for a moment before he answered Jack.

"We have to know the professor's exact location before we can continue this mission. If we're going to initiate a surprise attack, it's vital we snatch him as quickly as possible, and complete the extraction. Does Intel have any up to date information on the location?"

"They're working on that right now, J.D." Jack replied, "They're also trying to figure out how the Russians are going to move him. All they know is that troop carrier helo that is with the Black Shark helos has a lot of activity going on around it. Satellite photos show some sort of vehicle cargo is being removed from the helo, and being taken to a flat area adjacent to the helo. the guys are attaching something to them, once they have the in position."

J.D. seemed a little puzzled.

"Can you describe what these vehicles look like?" he asked.

Jack looked at the satellite monitor.

"They look like some kind of dune buggy, with an extended back section." Jack answered.

J.D. turned and looked at 'Bagger'.

"Dune gliders!" J.D. exclaimed. "That's how they're going to get out of there! "Those vehicles are ultralights. The ones they'll be using will be the two seater type. They can skirt the desert floor, or use the on board engine to traverse the terrain. The vehicle isn't easily spotted by radar. Our people wouldn't take notice of it. The vehicles themselves probably have modified engines that allow for long flights or ground travel. Either way, they'll escape if we don't get to them first."

Jack came back on line.

"My guess," said Jack, "is that the dune gliders will head toward the middle of Egypt, pass over the Sinai into Jordan, then fly north into Syria. It's a long haul, but those vehicles will be hard to detect. Fuel depots have probably been placed at strategic points to insure the completion of the mission."

J.D., Can your team be ready to lift off in five minutes?" Jack asked.

"The Ghost Shadow helos are still on the pads, ready to go." J.D. replied

"All tell the brass we're going forward with the mission," Jack said. "Hold on a minute, J.D., Intel just gave us the professors position. I'll transmit the coordinates to you, and you can get your team moving."

Jack looked at the Intel report in front of him.

"J.D.," Jack began, "The professor is being held in the basement of a building on the northeast side. 'There are 12 guards in the building and six on the outside. Any problem with that, J.D.?"

"Naw," J.D. came back. "It'll be like taking the Extraction 101 course again."

Jack just laughed and signed off.

Chapter 15

Desert Mission

J.D. and his Spec-Ops team headed for the main flight deck where the Ghost Shadow Squadron helos were located, and each squad boarded their assigned helo. The squawk box sounded: 'ATTENTION ALL SHIP'S PERSONNEL. ATTENTION ALL SHIP'S PERSONNEL... PREPARE TO LAUNCH HELOS ON MAIN FLIGHT DECK... HELOS BEGIN ROTATION.'

The blades of the stealth helos began to turn, picking up speed with each rotation until lift-off speed rotation was achieved. Once more, the Ghost Shadow Squadron was headed into harrm's way and the completion of another mission.

'LAUNCH PAD ALPHA... PREPARE TO LAUNCH HELO... LAUNCH. LAUNCH... LAUNCH...' came the command from the squawk. One by one, the helos headed down range. The AWACs aircraft was on station supplying radar cover. Operation Blue Light was once again a 'go'

The helos flew low, avoiding Egyptian and Libyan radar, came in east of Tobruk, heading for the mission target area.

As the rescue team headed toward the target, The Enterprise battle group was monitoring the Russian battle group. Captain Richard Hastings was on the bridge of the Enterprise, Admiral Mark Hewett's Flagship in the battle group. Hastings was receiving constant updates on the movement of the Russians.

"Captain," Commander Jim Johnson, the Executive Officer, said as he handed Hastings updated reports. "You might want to look at this latest configuration on the position the surface craft of the Russians. Notice that the heavy crafts are BEHIND this particular ship," pointing to the ship in the photograph, "which is a landing ship tank craft of some type. The front of the craft appears to have clam shell doors on the bow. Why would that type of craft be forward of the main body of warships?"

Hastings studied the photograph carefully.

"It might be to pick up Goldschmidt once they move him to a set location. I don't see why they would need such a large ship to pick up Goldschmidt from what will be a high speed transport craft. What's the present location of the Russians?"

"Fifteen thousand yards northeast of our current position, sir," Commander Johnson replied, "They're paralleling our current heading."

As Captain Hastings continued to contemplating what was going on with the Russians, the Ghost Shadow Squadron helos were descending on the landing zone about two clicks from the building where Goldschmidt was being held. J.D. 's squads quickly disembarked, once the helos touched down, and headed for the target building.

The squads were preparing to assault the building when Vertof exited the building and called to the perimeter guards.

"Red Palace just gave us the 'go' to start transport. Everybody back to the aircraft."

J.D. picked up the SAT phone and keyed in his team's frequency.

"All squads. abort the assault," he said, "We're going to follow these guys out to the landing field where those dune-gliders are... Back to the helos."

Vertov's men loaded Goldschmidt into the middle truck and the convoy moved out across the desert in the direction of the landing strip. Little did they know that J.D. and his team were right behind them, flying low.

The dune-gliders were set up and ready to take off by the time the convoy reached the landing strip. Goldschmidt was placed in the lead dune-glider, contemplating what his fate would be. Here was a man who had worked his way up in the field of physics to a PhD and beyond, always trying to find ways for mankind to improve on previous accomplishments in all fields, and to learn to apply these accomplishments to benefit, and not destroy mankind.

He thought back to the time he had made the breakthrough in laser technology and the effect it had on the many fields of science. Modern weaponry was only one accomplishment. Modifications of certain stages of the 'Cobalt Blue' process could be used in metallurgy, in medicine for the treatment of diseases such as cancer, in security systems. His contribution to the fields in science were tremendous.

'How will I be remembered in history?' he thought. 'Will it be as the inventor of destructive devices, or as a facilitator of processes that benefit mankind? His imprint on history was still in the making and he wanted it to be for the better.

Vertof climbed in next to him. Six more dune-gliders were utilized as escorts. The UNSU-I coder was strapped into the second dune-glider. Each one headed for the long plain ahead, and took off in tandem. Once they were airborne, they headed east for the Sinai desert. The Ghost Shadow Squadron began their pursuit.

The Ghost Shadow squadron followed the dune-gliders at an altitude five hundred feet above them. J.D. and the Alpha helo pilot kept studying the terrain as they flew. The dune-gliders would have to refuel at some point to refuel, and the Ghost Shadow helos would have to find a point close enough to approach them on the ground.

After two hours of flying, the dune-gliders began to descend and landed on the northeastern side of a wadi, a driedup creek bed in the desert, sometimes associated with an oasis. About one hundred feet from the landing site were old fortifications. The soldiers exited the dune-gliders and went into the first building, returning with gas cans and began to refuel the aircraft. Goldschmidt was allowed to leave his craft to stretch his legs. The wadi had an oasis about fifty feet from the buildings. Goldschmidt wondered down to the water pool to refresh himself from the heat.

The Ghost Shadow helos had held back and landed about two hundred yards to the west, behind a large sand dune. The Spec-Ops team disembarked and followed in a triad formation up the slope and took positions behind at the top of the dune.

Darkness was beginning to blanket the desert. The Spec-Ops team put their night vision goggles on.

J.D. hand signaled his team where the squads were to position themselves.

The squads moved out to the assigned positions and carefully made their way the slope toward the fortifications. J.D.'s Squad I would take out the lead dune-glider and extract Goldschmidt and remove the coding box from the number two dune-glider. Squad 2 would work its way behind the fortifications and neutralize any hostiles. Squads 3 and 4 would take up positions at the entrance to the buildings.

J.D. spotted Vertof next to his dune-glider, but Goldschmidt was not with him. He had gone down to the oasis before J.D. had gotten into position. J.D. hesitated and decided to take Vertof out with his tranquilizer gun. He moved silently placed himself behind a bush a short distance from Vertof and fired a tranquilizer dart into his neck. Within seconds, Vertofwas unconscious on the ground.

J.D. motioned to 'Bagger' to help him move Vertof out of sight. Once he was out of sight, J.D. radioed the Command Center and requested another helo be put on stand-by for the extraction. In the meantime, the guards returned with Goldschmidt. They seemed puzzled the Vertof was nowhere to be seen. Looking around, the one guard noticed a boot protruding from a bush a short distance from the dune-glider. The guard motioned to the other guard and raised their AK-47 assault rifles and proceeded toward the bush. J.D. and 'Bagger' dropped both of them with tranquilizer darts.

"'Swamp Rat' 5" J.D. whispered, "You and 'Bagger' take the big guy (Vertof) back to my helo. Take the lap-top he has and grab that code box from the dune-glider. We want both along with Goldschmidt."

Rat-a-tat-tat! Rat-a-tat-tat! All around them, Squad 3 heard the blast of machine gun fire ripping open the silent night. A hostile had spotted Squad 3 towards the back of the buildings and had open fired. Squad 3 had returned fire, and lobbed two percussion grenades into the hostile's position. More of the hostiles had moved toward Squad 3 because Squad 4 had moved in behind them and was catching them in a cross fire. Within minutes, all hostiles had been neutralized.

"Squads 3 and 4, light up those dune-gliders." J.D. yelled as the team began withdrawing." Get back to the helos. Dust-off in five minutes."

The Ghost Shadow helos were launch ready as the team scrambled over the top of the dune and down the other side with the men and equipment they were extracting. Vertof was placed on the Alpha helo and Goldschmidt and the coding box was placed on Beta helo. The helos began to lift off, and as they cleared the lift off zone. they were fired upon by two half-track trucks with cannons on them, which had come swooping across the desert. A shell exploded near the right tail section of Alpha helo, making it spin downward and to the right. The Alpha pilot wrestled with the controls and was able to regain control and stop the spin, then headed skvward.

'Who are THOSE guys ?" the pilot yelled back to J.D.

"l have no idea," J.D. responded. I thought we were the only ones out here besides the Russians."

Beta and Charlie helos went on the attack and fired four air-to-ground missiles at the trucks and blew them to pieces. The helos returned to the formation and headed back to the carrier.

Chapter 16

Peril at Sea...

While the Ghost Shadow helos were retuning from the mission, both the Russian and United States battle groups were closing on each other. Only six miles of water separated them. There appeared to be an emanate confrontation on the horizon. Suddenly there was an emergency SAT scramble on the bridge of the Enterprise.

"This is Eagle Eye with Flash Traffic for Falcon Nest... Four unknown aircraft heading northeast at fourteen thousand feet... Speed is Mach I .5... Unknowns heading towards both battle groups and are fifty nautical miles away... No weapon activation alarms from the unknowns at this time..."

"Acknowledged," Captain hasting replied.

"BATTLE STATIONS. BATTLE STATIONS... ALL P-ERSONNEL TO BATTLE STATIONS." blasted over the squawk box on the Enterprise.

Hastings climbed into the command chair and issued orders to the communications officer,

"Have the airborne alert aircraft maintain cover positions and prepare for confrontation."

Eagle Eye watched on radar as the unknowns shifted their flight path towards the Russians.

"Falcon Nest ... Unknown aircraft are Israeli FB-2s. FB-2s have dropped to one-hundred feet and are maintaining Mach 1.5 speed..."

Two of the FB-2s began their run between the heavy cruiser and the aircraft carrier, still not in attack mode.

The heavy cruiser and the aircraft carrier slowed forward speed and maintained course. As the FB-2 aircraft approached the Russian ships, the AWACs aircraft noticed several scoop-shaped antennae moving up from below the Russian ship's main decks, each pointed in the path of the incoming aircraft.

One of the FB-2's swooped between the two ships and appeared to go through some type of atmospheric distortion, which affected the United States aircraft also, especially their compasses. The FB-2 began to stall out as it attempted a steep climb skyward, and began dropping altitude. All of its electronics became intermittent and shut down. All communications equipment fell silent. The pilot, Major Zev Bresler, watch stopped, and he became dizzy and woozy, but he managed to land his aircraft on the water. He pushed the self- destruct button on the control panel to prevent capture of the aircraft be the Russians. Nothing happened. The aircraft was floating on the water. The pilot managed to manually open the cockpit canopy and escaped down the side to the right wing.

"The Russians must have hit that aircraft with a concentrated ray of electromagnetic radiation pulse!" Captain Hastings exclaimed.

Major Bresler, surveyed the situation around him. Four Russian fast attack surface craft had surrounded his aircraft, and divers from those surface craft were attaching flotation devices to the FB-2 to prevent it from sinking. Bresler, as a last resort to avoid capture of him and his aircraft, pulled out his flare gun, and fired a flare toward the fuel cell behind the wing. Due to the pitch of the aircraft and the angle of the shot, the flare was deflected, and went into the sea.

The LSD salvage craft headed over to the downed aircraft and pilot and opened its bow clam-shell doors.

Bresler was in a hazy mental state and became disoriented. Russian divers pulled him off the wing and loaded him into one of the fast attack surface craft. The divers then returned to the water to assist with the flotation devices being attached to the FB-2.

The remaining FB-2s shot skyward and looped to return to the downed aircraft's position. The Russian's battle group and the ship which was loading the downed aircraft and pilot were to close to risk firing a missile without the situation exploding into a major confrontation.

As the Russians proceeded with their loading process, the United States battle group had come within four nautical miles of the Russians. Captain Hastings contacted the Russian battle group commander and requested their intentions.

"We are involved in a rescue mission and salvage process of the pilot and his aircraft." The Russian commander replied. "We have the situation in hand and do not require any assistance from your group." The Russians terminated any further transmission.

Admiral Hewett, Deputy of Naval Operations in the Mediterranean addressed Captain Hastings. "Captain, contact the Joint Chiefs in Washington, explain the situation and request suggestions on how to resolve this without a shooting confrontation."

"Contact Washington, Jim," Captain Hastings told his Executive Officer, "and see what action they want us to take."

"Yes, Captain," Jim replied. "Are we going to hold at our current position?"

Captain Hastings frowned. "Looks like we have no choice at the moment."

The remaining formation of FB-2's made one more pass OVER the Russian battle group but out of the range of the EMR equipment, showing no hostile intent, shot skyward, and disappeared into the clouds.

Jack Logan was standing in the Ready Response Center, watching the actions occurring in the Mediterranean on the monitor displays when a Flash message came across the monitor. It was from Captain Hastings on the Enterprise.

'The Russians have just snagged an Israeli FB-2 and its pilot... Israelis so far not responding. The Russians will stall for time so they can examine the FB-

They will want to know about its new propulsion system and high speed maneuverability.

The phone next to Jack began ringing. He picked up the receiver and identified himself. "Jack Logan." It was the CIA with more information on the Mediterranean situation. The CIA had intercepted a message from Israel to the Russian commander of the battle group.

Can you put that up on the display monitor?" Jack asked. The person on the other end of the line complied and the message was placed on the monitor.

The message read:

'Attention, Russian battle group commander. This is the Israeli Air Defense Minister, General Josef. You have downed one of our aircraft in international air space, and have detained the pilot as well as salvaged the aircraft. We demand that you return the aircraft and the pilot to us immediately. If you do not comply, we have no choice but to obtain what is ours by force. Respond.'

The Russian battle group responded.

'Mister Defense Minister, the aircraft of which you speak has no identifying markings on it. The aircraft approached our battle group in a threatening manner and we were merely defending our ships. If you will contact our defense minister in Moscow, we can perhaps resolve this situation to our mutual satisfaction. We will keep the aircraft and its pilot in the meantime.'

The situation was no longer an incident. It was turning into a major crisis. Captain Hastings initiated battle protocol for the group and kept on course heading parallel with the Russian ships.

Chapter 17

Showdown

The White House Rapid Response Center was teaming with activity since the Russians had removed the downed FB-2 from the sea and taken the pilot to the command ship for interrogation. With the intel he had seen on the display monitor, the Israeli government was intent on its demand for the release of the pilot and return of the aircraft. Diplomacy was now the order of the day, and the Russian Ministry of Defense was in contact with the Israeli Defense Force Minister. Israel directed a point that the Russian salvage ship would sail too. The ship would also have the pilot on board to be returned to his country.

The Russians were attempting to use stall tactics, to gain the upper hand. They told the Israelis that they would have to meet with them at a neutral spot, and discuss the plans for the return of pilot and aircraft.

Jack's SAT phone beeped. He picked up the phone and responded. It was J.D.

"What's the situation over there? "Jack asked. "We're getting all kinds of intel on a pending confrontation between the Russians and the Israelis."

"Jack," answered J.D. "The main objective of the Russian operation was to capture an FB-2. When they heard Vertof had kidnapped Goldschmidt, they knew he would try and ransom him. The Russians decided to use the ransom ploy to their advantage and bid on Goldschmidt to get him out in the open. The Russians knew that the Israeli government would send a ground and air force to intercept the kidnappers, and give the Russians a chance to bring down an FB-2 over the Mediterranean Sea. They sent a battle group whose ships contained a new ESR pulse ray weapon. The pulse ray has a limited range, so they had to lure the FB-2 close to the surface ships to get a shot in. It worked. The FB-2 was hit from both sides and crashed into the sea. All the Russians had to do was pick up the aircraft and pilot."

"We captured Vertof, and he has enough information in the computer he had with him to topple the Russian government. It contains all VertoPs contacts, his business connections, his military connections, and who's on the payroll in the Kremlin. It's the 'Holy Grail' of Russian socioeconomic structure. We have what we went in for and are heading back to Eagle's Nest."

"That's not the half of it, J.D." Jack replied, "Israel has threatened to stop the Russians from returning to Russia with the aircraft and its pilot. If they try and make good on that threat, The United States is going to have to back them up. Our government is trying to negotiate a solution between Russia and Israel, but it may take some time.'

-D. thought for a moment, then responded.

"Jack, I have an idea that might defuse the crisis," said J.D.

What ever you have, let's hear it," said Jack, "We're willing to anything at this point. The last thing we want is a shooting war."

J.D. outlined a plan to resolve the crisis as Jack wrote down the highlights. Once Jack had all the necessary information, he signed off with J.D. and went across the room to the President and his advisors had gathered.

Jack approached President Steele.

"I think there might be a solution to this crisis, Mr. President." Jack began. "J.D. 's team have checked the computer that Vertof had with him. They have cracked the encryption code and analyzed the data. It contains the whole structure of his organization, including his contacts in the Russian infrastructure. We should be able to negotiate a trade between the Russians and Israelis by offering to turn over Vertof and his computer for the Israeli aircraft and its pilot, Major Bresler."

"If that computer contains the information you say it does, I'd say we keep it for our own security," the President said, "Besides, if we return Vertof and the computer, the Russians have got to know we copied what was on the computer."

"You have a point, Mr. President," Jack said, "but we must think of the current situation. On the one hand, we have enough information on the Russians to push the balance of power in our direction, but on the other hand, we have the distinct possibility of an all-out nuclear confrontation. I propose, Mr. President that we present this proposal to the Russians and the Israelis to end this crisis. Having the balance of power shift in our direction is indeed a positive solution for the United States, but if we exchange it for a peaceful resolution, and it prevents a nuclear confrontation, then I do not feel we have a choice."

The President and his advisors sat down at the conference table measuring the pros and cons of the proposal. Finally, after thirty minutes of discussion, all were in agreement.

"Get the Russian President Zorkoff and the Israeli Prime Minister Cohen on the hot line and end this." The President ordered, looking at the monitor displays. "We'll see if this is agreeable to both sides."

The hot line rang in the Russian President's office in the Kremlin and in the Israeli Prime Minister's office in Tel Aviv. Once both leaders were on the line, The President of the United States explained what the United States proposed to resolve the current stand-off between Russia and Israel.

"Where and when would the exchange take place?" asked President Zorkoff, "and what assurances that the United States and Israel will honor this proposal?"

"You have my word as President of the United States," said President Steele," that this proposal will be honored by both our countries. We are aware of the importance of Vertof is to your government. We propose that the exchange take place on the USS Enterprise. Your government may send a helicopter transport to return Major Bresler and in return Vertof to your battle group. The Israeli government is sending a naval vessel to retrieve the aircraft. As a gesture of good faith, our battle group forces will withdraw from the USS Enterprise and station the ships at a point agreed upon. We request that you, also, order your forces to stand down. All of the USS Enterprise fighter wing will stand down. The Israeli government naval forces will be placed along the side the Russian salvage ship, and take part in the transfer of the downed aircraft to the Israeli salvage ship. Once the transfer is completed, all naval vessels will withdraw from the area. The exchange will begin as soon as possible, once the agreement is confirmed."

There was a moment's pause in the conversation.

"I must confer with my military advisors before any agreement is reach." Said President Zorkoff." I will call you as soon as there is a resolution agreed upon.'

Both men placed their receivers back in their cradles.

Finally, after several minutes passed, a favorable response from the Kremlin came over the hot line. The Russians agreed to the proposal.

The Israeli naval vessel was prepared to move to the assigned location for the transfer. but were still intent on using force if necessary.

Captain Hastings on the Enterprise was informed as to the placement of his ship and the placement of the rest of the battle group, and the Russian's agreement to stand down their their military forces.

Chapter 18

The Transfer and Prelude to War

The Israeli retrieval vessel had already put to sea and was approaching the Russian salvage vessel from the southeast. Bothe the Russian and United States battle groups had taken a 'stand down' position, leaving only the Enterprise in an isolated area. A helicopter had been dispatched from the Russian aircraft carrier with Major Bresler aboard, to the Enterprise. Vertof was being prepped for his return to the Russians.

In the sick bay of the Enterprise, J.D. and the Executive Officer of the Enterprise observed as the Chief Medical Officer for the ship injected Vertof with a special tranquilizer drug that would allow him to speak, but he could not focus on the conversation.

The Israeli ship positioned itself to initiate the transfer of the downed aircraft from the Russian ship to the Israeli ship. As the aircraft was being lowered into the Israeli vessel, the enterprise sonar picked up a high speed whirring sound, tracking towards the Israeli vessel.

"Captain Hastings!" yelled the sonar technician, "High speed screws, probably a torpedo, heading toward the salvage craft! Impact in 25 seconds!"

"Who the hell fired that torpedo?!" Hastings yelled back.

Second set of screws following one hundred yards behind the first on, sir," The sonar technician replied.

Hastings quickly look at the positions of the ships in his battle group. He grabbed the radio microphone and transmitted to his closest destroyer.

"Enterprise to DD Mason, can you take out those torpedoes before they hit their targets."

"Not both of them, Captain, but we can kill the first one." came the response from the destroyer.

The Mason immediately launched its own guided torpedo on an intercept course with the hostile torpedo.

Things were heating up on the bridge of the Enterprise. The Russians had monitored the firing of the torpedo also, and radioed the Enterprise.

"Is this how you keep your word!?" The Russian Commander yelled over the radio.

"That wasn't from our group that initiated the torpedo launch!" Hastings responded.

The rogue torpedo was rapidly closing on the Israeli vessel, which was trying to take evasive action. The torpedo fired from the Mason was locked on and closing on its target. Intercept and detonation occurred two hundred feet from the Israeli vessel. The second torpedo was on course and headed for the bow of the ship. Suddenly, a stream of high intensity light struck the water just ahead of the second torpedo, detonating the torpedo's warhead. Someone in the War Room, deep in the underground of the Pentagon had activated one of the laser satellites.

"... Two fish dead in the water, Captain!" yelled the sonar technician.

The Russians radioed the Enterprise they had nothing to do with the firing of the torpedoes, and requested the exchange continue.

Both sides agreed and Major Bresler was now on board the Enterprise and Anatoly Vertof, with his computer, was on the helo headed for the Russian aircraft carrier.

Once the Russian helo was off the deck, Captain Hastings issued orders to his Air Wing.

He announced action over the squawk box.

"... ATTENTION ENTERPRISE AIR WING. REACTIVATE NOW!...NOW!...NOW!...FOUR READY ALERT AIRCRAFT

RETURN TO TAKE-OFF POSITIONS AND PREPARE TO LAUNCH… A-5 FLIGHT REFUELERS, GO TO LAUNCH POSITIONS…"

The flight deck became a bee hive of activity as deck hands and flight crews hurried to their assigned duties.

Both the Russian and the United States battle groups moved back into their original course and heading.

As the battle groups were repositioning, the sonar technician on the Enterprise yelled out.

"High speed screws targeting the Enterprise, thirty degrees stern, Captain! Estimated impact in thirty seconds! …"

The DD -Mason was on the left stern of the Enterprise, and moved at flank speed to cross the wake of the Enterprise.

"Attention all hands!" yelled Captain Orizano of the Mason." Sound collision alarm!… Torpedo tracking us instead of the Enterprise!'

Back on the Enterprise, four F-14's had launched and were airborne.

The diverted torpedo caught up to the Mason, and detonated producing a gaping hole in her stern. Escort ships rushed to the Mason to assist in rescue and damage control.

Jack was viewing what was happening on the monitors on satellite up-link in the Ready Response Room in Washington. As he watched, both battle groups were maneuvering into conflict configuration. Both groups had aircraft in the air and the destroyers and heavy cruisers were turning to engage the enemy. As he continued to watch, Jack saw two explosions occur to the south of the conflict area. A Flash message came over the printer from the War Code Scrambler: Russian submarine, under control of a captain loyal to Vertof, destroyed. Russian government did NOT order the attack… Repeat, Russian Government did NOT order the attack! … Verify receipt of this Flash message on FTC-101 (Flash traffic coder).

The DEFCON board over the monitors was reading DEFCON 2. It wouldn 't be long before it would go to DEFCON l, total commitment. President Steele was on the Hot Line to President Zorkoff in the Kremlin, desperately trying to avert a thermonuclear war.

"I just received word that the attack on the Israeli vessel was not ordered by your government, President Zorkoff," President Steele said, "I've ordered our battle group to stand down and withdraw from the area. I'm requesting you follow my lead."

President Zorkoff surveyed his monitors. After a moment of silence, he responded to President Steele.

"I concur with the decision," President Zorkoff said. "I will give the order to my forces to stand dovm."

Both sides had received casualties in men and equipment as the two presidents of the superpowers were negotiating. Several Russian MIG 21 's and United States F-14's were destroyed in dog fights and the destroyers on both sides had inflicted main hits on the opposing sides. The Israeli FB-2's were the only aircraft left in the sky, once the stand down order was given to both combatants. The FB-2's continued their protective posturing over the Israeli salvage ship.

Back in Washington, Jack sank back into his chair and continued surveying the monitors for any additional activity. Suddenly, a bomber appeared on the radar consoles of both battle groups, and on the monitor in the Rapid Response Room. As the bomber approached the area of original confrontation, the bomber dropped a cruise missile from its undercarriage. Both battle groups responded as an aggressive move from the opposite side. In the Rapid Response Room, the DEFCON board went to DEFCON 1. World War III was about to begin. All monitor boards and the main War Board lit up with nuclear missile pre-launch information in the United States as well as Russia.

Jack stared at the array of data on the monitors in disbelief. Who had launched the missile that would carry the world into Armageddon? And Why?

"No!" Jack yelled as he ran toward the secured lines at the back of the room.

While running, Jack fell over a chair and banged his head on the conference table. Everything went black. Jack fell into a state of unconsciousness.

It seemed like an endless amount of time passed before Jack began coming out of his unconsciousness. Jack slowly opened his eyes, and looked around at his surroundings. Chris was standing next to the bed with neurologists and other medical staff, and he realized he was no longer in the Ready Response Room. All around the room were pieces of equipment he did not recognize, and what appeared to be technicians observing the data on the equipment. Jack was at a total loss as to what was happening.

"Are you Okay, Jack?" Chris asked him. "You've been out for about four hours."

"What is this place?" asked Jack. "The last thing I remember I was running toward the back of the Ready Response Room, tripped and fell, and hit my head. I know the 'Big Board' was at DEFCON 1 I…I don't know what happened after that."

Chris looked down at his brother.

"You were never in the Rapid Response Room, Jack. Don't you remember that you were working with Professor Goldschmidt on the virtual reality project that would give a 'live' scenario that you would have to respond to? You've been working for the past four days on it. You volunteered to act as the 'Guinee pig' for testing the feasibility of the different scenarios we might have to face in the future. You never left this testing lab. There apparently was something that happened in your brain to cause you to get up and try to run. The virtual reality team is working on the problem. And, by the way, the project was a success. All the data collected seems to fall in line with what Professor Goldschmidt initially theorized as responses."

Jack slowly sat up on the bed.

"Then none of this was real?" Jack asked.

"None of it." Responded Chris." I've been over at the missile center working with NASA on the new configurations for the Four Apostles satellites, while you were 'cruising in dreamland'.

"Then I'm not head of CIA in the Middle East?" Jack asked quietly.

"Sorry Jack. but you're going to have to wait a while to see that pay-grade."

Chris said placing his hand on Jack's shoulder. "I brought your other suit from your locker. We have that final conference at NASA at 0900 hours and it's 0700

Hours now. You can shower in the annex and get dressed. I'll meet you in front of the building in about forty-five minutes."

"Are you sure you're all right, Jack?" Chris asked as he turned to leave.

They want you to go to the hospital for a day or two to have some tests run, then you can go home."

Jack just stared out into space and answered, "Sure. I'm all right. I can't wait to get home… See you in forty-five minutes…"

Chapter 19

Chris Returns Home

Chris's government jet touched down at 2:25 PM at Pittsburgh International Airport. He was a bit exhausted from the four day briefing with Professor Goldschmidt and NASA officials. The jet taxied to an area just below the main concourse. Chris gathered his carry-on baggage and deplaned. He walked across the tarmac to a security door, entered the terminal and walked up the steps to the main concourse. He was having trouble balancing his baggage as he headed toward the entrance of the terminal, which lead to the parking area. Halfway to the terminal entrance, he had to go off to the side and sit down on a bench that was across from the Oklahoma Western Airways counter. He fumbled with the baggage for a moment, looking down to make sure everything was where he wanted it, and rose from the seat. As Chris stood up, his eyes caught a glimpse of someone he recognized standing in front of the Arrival/Departure board at the ticket counter. It was Elise! What Chris didn't know was Elise had been visiting her parents and was on her way back to Tucson, Arizona.

Chris couldn't believe it! He hadn't seen or had contact with her for the past twenty years, and now she was standing about twenty-five feet away. His mind whirled, trying to decide if he should walk over to her, or simply walk away.

Fate intervened. Elise had turned away from the board and her eyes met his. Elise's jaw dropped slightly, and she stood there frozen in the moment. Chris set his baggage down and slowly walked toward her. Elise remained unmoving. At last they stood inches from each other. Their eyes were transfixed on one another. Feelings flowed back and forth between them as they had in the years of their youth. Nothing was said at first. Time stopped, and the two of them searched each other's souls' through this moment in eternity. Finally, Chris spoke. His voice was slightly cracking from the emotions he was feeling.

"Elise," he began, then paused. "It's been so long... How... How are you?"

Elise just stood there, unable to speak, wondering what to say.

Chris... What... What are you doing here? ... How long were you standing over there?."

Chris wanted to take her in his arms and return to the time when it was just Chris and Elise, but he knew all to well what was reality.

"I... I just flew back from Washington D.C..."

Elise, in her heart, wanted what Chris wanted, to feel the warm embrace and caring touch, bringing back to her all that they had shared. She wanted the kiss she knew so well when they had been apart for a while, the slow soft kiss that finished with the passion that they, alone, shared in their hearts.

"I... I don't know what to say, Chris... It's been so long. Where do I start?"

Chris tried to put her at ease.

Chris cleared his throat. "You can ask me if I missed you, like you use to do... Maybe that will help..."

Elise smiled and seemed to relax. She tilted her head the way she always had done before. "Miss. me?" she asked.

Chris delayed answering for a short moment.

"Yes,... Every moment we've been apart. You've never left me..."

Chris took Elise by the hand and they walked over to the bench where Chris had been sitting.

Elise looked down as they sat facing each other.

"Why now, Chris?... Why did we have to see each other now? ... I'm living in Tucson, Arizona. I have a husband and two children and have a very happy life. I'm working as an orthopedic surgical scrub nurse. but with all that's right in my life, I. I've never forgotten what we had together."

Chris placed his hand on her shoulder and Elise raised her head until their eyes met once more.

"I'm married, too, Elise… to a wonderful woman. and we have two children. I've been working in the medical field and teaching in medical technical schools. I still work with computer systems, just to keep up in the field. A situation came up in the systems I worked with in the military and I was 'drafted into participating."

Chris paused for a moment and placed her hands in his.

"I read the poems I wrote for you… and I go back to OUR time I can't let go either."

Just then, the loud speaker interrupted their conversation.

'Oklahoma Western Airlines now announcing final call for Flight 54 for Oklahoma City, Tucson, and Los Angeles…'

Elise rose from the bench.

"That's my flight… I have to go." Elise said.

Chris stood up, not wanting them to part so soon. He slowly put his arms around her, and tried to kiss her. Elise pulled away slightly.

"I can't. I can't, Chris. I'm sorry… I don't want any more confusion in my life. It isn't that I don't want to, it's just that…"

Chris released his embrace and stepped back. He understood. They were living different lives, and neither wanted to hurt those now in their lives.

"Have you. thought… of us at all, over the years?" Chris asked.

"Yes," was Elise's immediate response. "I think about us every day. I kept the poems you wrote for me… And I read and re-read them whenever I can."

"I'm sorry I didn't get back in time for me to exchange my wings for a diamond ring." Chris said softly.

Elise looked deeply into Chris's eyes. "Our love is too strong for me to just let it go, even though I married someone else." Elise replied, wiping away a tear.

Again, the loud speaker interrupted… 'Attention pleases. All passengers for Oklahoma Western Flight 54… Final call for departure. All passengers should be on board…'

Elise turned to walk toward the gate, and looked back at Chris.

"Always remember Chris, those words from your one poem to me. 'You are me… And I am you… What we are, we are together'

Good-by, my love…" She headed toward the departure gate. She didn't look back.

Chris watched her as she entered the departure gate area and disappeared. The void he had felt in his heart in the past on the day he received her last letter returned to haunt him. He walked back to where he had dropped his baggage, picked it up, and headed for the terminal entrance. His eyes moistened as he walked. All at once, he heard a voice calling to him.

"Chris!… Chris!… Please wait!… Chris!… Wait!" It was Elise.

Chris looked back down the concourse and saw Elise running toward him. He dropped his baggage and turned and ran toward her. They met each other with open arms, and embraced each other as they had each time they were together so long ago. Their souls once more came alive as they kissed with the passion that was theirs and made them one.

Elise was quietly crying, tears gently dropping from her eyes.

"Chris… Darling… I love you so much. I wish it was our time to be together… Don't stop loving me… Our time will come. I believe that. …

She left Chris's embrace and rushed back to catch her plane. Chris just stood there and watched. She was gone. Twice in his life he had lost her. If there would ever be another time, he would not let it happen again. For now, it was time to return to the real world. Jessie was waiting for him at home. It was going to be a long drive, but it would give him time to ponder the feelings within.

Elise entered the Departure Waiting Area and walked to the boarding ramp, showed her boarding pass, and boarding pass, and boarded the plane, turning to the left and moved forward to her seat in the first class section. Her seat number was B l, a window seat. She placed her carry-on luggage in the compartment above her seat and moved to her assigned seat. As usual, she sat down and placed her legs under her. She looked out the window, her mind trying to gather together all the unanswered questions about what had just occurred between her and Chris.

The cabin entrance door was shut and locked by the flight attendant. The engines began to whine as each was brought on line, and the plane began to slowly back away from the dock. The plane began moving forward toward the runway, and Elise looked out of her window and saw Chris walking to the parking lot. The departing plane reminded her of her last letter to Chris, in which she described a scenario from a television series concerning two lovers whose destiny was much like theirs. 'What will OUR outcome be?' Elise thought to herself as the plane reached the runway, began its forward momentum in its ascent to the sky. In a few short moments, the plane had disappeared into the clouds.

As Chris reached his car, he remembered the last letter Elise had written. He looked up into the sky and saw a passenger jet climbing into the clouds. Perhaps it was Elise's jet. In his mind, it fit the situation that something always kept interfering with their plans to be together. He unlocked his car, placed the baggage in the back seat, got in behind the steering wheel, paused for a moment, and started the car. He left the parking lot and headed for home.

An hour later, Chris turned off the gravel road in front of his house and drove up the driveway, parking next to Jessie's car. Jessie came out of the house and walked toward Chris as he got out his car and collected his baggage. Chris met her halfway, and they embraced and held each other.

"Chris. What's going on? Two FBI agents came to my workplace and told me that I had to go with them, that it concerned you and some kind of special mission you had to carry out in Washington, D.C., but they couldn't tell me what it was. When we got to where we were going, Joe and Kim were there too. The one agent explained that we had to go to a safe house until you completed your mission."

Chris and Jessie walked on up to the front door.

"I'll explain what I can, Jessie, but it won't be much," Chris said, "Most of it has to do with national security and a project I worked on while I was in the Air Force."

Jessie stopped before they opened the front door and turned toward Chris.

"It didn't involve. Elise… Did it?" She asked. He had discussed his relationship Elise with Jessie, but left certain things out.

Chris looked directly into Jessie's eyes and sighed.

"No. Jess… Elise wasn't involved…

Jessie looked back into Chris's eyes and then looked toward the ground.

"I'm sorry, Chris… When something like this happens, I'm always afraid that someway, somehow, Elise has re-entered your life. I guess I'll never really believe she's gone from your memory, and you only love me."

Chris's thoughts went back to that chance meeting with Elise at the airport. He had to reassure Jessie everything between them was all right.

"You don't have to worry, Jess," he said, "It's you and me, together…

Ok?"

Jessie looked reassured as they entered their home, and things were settled.

Both of their children were at Jessie's parents for the evening and Jessie and Chris had a quiet supper together. After dinner, Chris told Jessie he was going to take a walk. He left the house, walked down the driveway, across the road to the field with the big oak tree on a small rise in the pasture, to relax from the past several days work on the Four Apostles Project. The oak tree was his favorite place of solitude. It always brought him peace of mind, and though he didnt know it then, it would be a place of a new beginning in the future. Jessie understood his need to be by himself from time to time, just to gather his thoughts and reflect on things going on in his life.

Jessie watched Chris from the kitchen window as he strolled down the driveway. The sun was setting and the sky and the surrounding trees were alive with colorful hues. The evening breeze caused the orchard grass to flow gently back and forth. It was a beauty that one longs for when soul-searching in the heart.

Chris walked up the rise, and sat down under the swaying branches of the oak. He looked toward the sunset and thought about times of long ago and far awav. He remembered a certain nurse's ball, and how he lost the chance to be with the one person who was his forever love. Though he could not be with Elise, his feelings for her would always remain in his heart.

Chris leaned back against the tree, surrounding himself with memories, especially of his meeting with Elise that day. Jessie watched him from the window of their home.

'He's back... and he loves me,' Jessie thought as she gazed out the window, watching Chris settle beneath the oak tree. And the autumn sun slowly drifted toward the horizon, and night began to fall. Elise was now only a breath awav. But Jessie would never know.

Chapter 20

De' Jevu...

Jack had to go through a debriefing on the effects of his virtual reality experience, and was sent to the medical wing of the project for further testing. He had to stay in the medical wing for 2 days, and then was released, to return for further evaluation in four weeks. He had been away to long from his home and family. Jack planned an evening out with his wife, Cindy, and his children, Charlie and Charlene. but his experience had exhausted him, and he begged off for at least another day or two. Jack and Cindy decided to make an early night of it, and went to bed about nine o'clock that night.

The secure line next to his bed had a red button set into the base of the phone. The phone button would flash in time of crisis, as well ring, , and by pressing the button. the phone was automatically connected to the White House Rapid Response Center. It was 0200 hours when the line went hot. Jack, half asleep. reached over, picked up the receiver, and pushed the button.

"Jack Logan, ID 374," Jack said, having trouble believing he wasn't stuck in a dream or was suffering after effects from the virtual reality experience.

"Jerry Whitfield, ID 177," came the response, "President Steele has called a meeting on 'Operation Blue Light' , a rescue mission, in the Rapid Response Center ASAP. It appears the Four Apostles Project has been compromised. A coded message was sent to a terrorist group headquarters in Lebanon by one of their operatives in the United States and was intercepted by the CIA. The action mentioned in the message could completely destabilize the Middle East. The terrorists have kidnapped our top physicist on the Four Apostle Project. The briefing will start at 0300 hours. Better bring some coffee, Jack… It's going to be a long night.

With that, Jack hung up the receiver, wiped the sleep from his eyes, and got out of bed.

Jerry Whitfield, The White House Chief of staff, sounded forbodding, to say the least. Jack, as new Director of Middle East Strategic Operations Services Group, had only been briefed the day before. The preparation for the Four Apostles Project spanned almost two decades, and held the highest level of secrecy in the government. What Jack had been briefed on was just the tip of the iceberg. The level of information to be presented at this briefing was to be far and beyond what Jack expected.

Jack hurriedly dressed, and was slowly becoming aware of exactly what was happening. He kissed his wife on the forehead, and rushed down the stairs and out the door to his vehicle. The cool autumn air helped wake him up to the fact that he had just finished this scenario!

Was he acting out the virtual reality memories in his brain? Was this the REAL DEAL this time? What was going on? Was history leading to World War III about to change?

Jack knew this was no dream. Because his dream had been so vivis — so real Jack knew that this time the outcome would be different. The laws of time and space were subject to change, although just how, Jack didn't know. He just knew he would be a part of it.

And this time, he would stop Armageddon in its tracks!

The End -

www.ingramcontent.com/pod-product-compliance
Lightning Source LLC
Chambersburg PA
CBHW070452170726
48291CB00005B/1711
* 9 7 8 1 9 4 9 7 4 6 9 1 4 *